About the Author

Glenn Erik has previously published short fiction in *Bravado* and *Mindfood Magazine*. He has a Bachelor of Arts from Victoria University and currently resides in Dunedin, New Zealand. *Drunk before the Sun* is his debut novel.

Drunk Before the Sun

Glenn Erik

Drunk Before the Sun

Vanguard Press

VANGUARD PAPERBACK

© Copyright 2024
Glenn Erik

A CIP catalogue record for this title is
available from the British Library.

ISBN 978-1-83794-231-2

*Vanguard Press is an imprint of
Pegasus Elliot Mackenzie Publishers Ltd.*
www.pegasuspublishers.com

First Published 2024

**Vanguard Press
Sheraton House Castle Park
Cambridge England**

Printed & Bound in Great Britain

To Ian

I'd like to thank all those who read my first draft. Special thanks to Michael Welson who had the balls to point out its faults, and to Chris Else who showed me how to fix them. I'd also like to thank my wife for putting up with my mad obsessions.

1

November 26th, 2000

How long have I been dead to the world?

The engine has stopped.

Drool runs from the corner of my mouth.

I get out of the car, stretch, let the blood flow into my legs. It takes a moment to appreciate the amazing numbing effect in both my butt cheeks. A personal best. I really can't feel my arse.

I'm standing on the footpath in some derelict suburb – tagged fences, battered letterboxes, drab curtains pulled at the windows. Not exactly the destination I had in mind. At a guess it's late afternoon, hard to tell with the grey sky and how far south we've travelled. This could be Palmerston North, maybe even as far as Levin or Porirua. The biggest question though, where the hell is Lincoln?

I try not to sweat it. The keys are still in the ignition. He probably snuck off for a deal, likely in some tinny house right now. No point worrying. I hop back in the car, recline the seat and switch on the radio. Bon Jovi, *Livin' on a Prayer*, delivers a pang of 1980s' nausea. I quickly turn the dial, all the way to the end – just ads and crap music – then switch it off.

Waiting, watching the faulty clock flashing on the dashboard, gets me ruminating. Maybe this was why he wanted to come to Wellington? Lincoln must be dealing, I can't think of anything else. How long before I go searching, and even if that were wise I wouldn't know where to begin, which door to knock on.

Suddenly I hear him yelling my name.

I sit up.

Something has got him spooked. Up ahead, Lincoln's running in the middle of the road as if he's being chased down by a gunman. He glances over his shoulder, quickens his pace in a frantic rush for a try line. "Kurt, start the car!" There's so much strain carved into his face I can easily imagine it staying there permanently. He's gripping a blue sports bag, and as he nears, I see in fact… he *is* being chased by a gunman. This guy is big, as in blubbery big – a version of Jabba the Hutt swinging a sawn-off in his left.

Holy shit nuts! I shift into the driver's seat and turn the ignition, but haven't a clue how to drive manual. Gear, clutch, handbrake, check.

Lincoln yanks open the door, flies in throwing the bag in the back. "What the fuck! Drive!"

I floor the accelerator. Nothing happens. I'm pumping the clutch in a nervous frenzy. The gunman – long greasy hair, leather jacket, belly flopping all over the place – is almost within range. He lifts the sawn-off with one hand, aims.

Lincoln shifts the gear into reverse. I plant the throttle. Hurtling backwards, we duck as the first shot cracks the windscreen, showering us in glass. The car pulls sideways, hits the curb, my foot slips and we stall, breached on the road, vulnerable.

Lincoln tugs at me. "Get out! I'm driving!" As the gunman stops to reload, we do a lightening exchange of seats. Lincoln plants a wheel spinning U-turn. The guy raises his gun again, but we've got some distance now. *Boom*! The second shot sprays, cracks the rear window in a spidery web. The gunman's bent over, catching his breath, sawn-off resting at his side as we screech around the corner, out of sight.

"What the fuck, Lincoln? What the fuck, man? What the fuck?"

Lincoln doesn't answer. He remains silent, calm as a monk. He slows to a legal speed and finds the onramp to the motorway. I'm fighting down waves of nausea, perspiring nervous sweat, scanning my body for bullet holes – miraculously there are none. With a missing windscreen the wind pressure distorts our faces, morphs our eyes into kamikaze slits as we descend into the bowl of Wellington city. Lincoln cuts back the gears and sidles up cosy with the stationary traffic.

Great. Now we're a shiny cop magnet – an outdoor installation of criminal art. I look around, on edge. Crystals of glass litter the car, decorate my hair. You'd have to be a real idiot not to notice the smashed windows, front and back. We're reeling in looks from commuters – hook, line and sinker. Not that Lincoln's helping the matter – he's whipped out a toothbrush of all things and has begun brushing his teeth. A curious trait I've never quite got used to. No water, no toothpaste, just dry bristling, buffing up his pearly whites. It either helps him think or it's some kind of symptom of a severe hyperactivity disorder.

"Listen," he says, stalling with the brush in hand. "I know what you're thinking. But before I can answer any questions, we need to ditch the car, find somewhere private." He looks at me, seriously for once. "Okay?"

I laugh out of sheer nervousness. "And what do you think is going to keep me in this seat for another second. Tell me that?"

Lincoln sighs, produces a smile. "Look in the bag, Kurt. Just look in the bag." He continues his brushing. The lights change. We're moving again and perhaps I've lost my will to leave because when I unzip the bag thousands of faces of Queen Liz stare straight up at me.

2

For what it's worth, I never thought I would get involved in this stuff, but here I am – twenty-one years old, unemployed, staring at the contents of a bag resembling a life free from debt and a brain-dead job, and wondering why the shrapnel which flew past my head earlier felt more meaningful than all the lectures I've attended this year combined.

There is definitely something wrong with me.

It would be easy to blame my mother who kicked me out of home this morning, fuelling my sudden urge to leave Auckland, or perhaps completing my degree that has left me jobless and, frankly, lost. Maybe I've been living a predictable path around the sun far too long and just wanted to upset my orbit. Surely something from all this and the allure of the South Island and that it's summer and that I had nothing else better to do than accept a free ride from my drug dealer, can explain why I'm here?

We're sitting in a private room at a city backpacker. The door is locked, the sports bag slumped on the floor between us. I have to pinch myself. This is not some kind of joyride I could choose to step off later.

"Right, Lincoln. You need to tell me everything. How you got this, who this belongs to? Most of all, if we took this, decided to actually keep the money, would we be fucked?"

Lincoln doesn't look up – he's too focused on shaving his legs. "Of course we're going to keep it. What are you worried about?"

"Oh… perhaps violent retribution?"

He taps the razor against a bowl of hot water, casually glances up at me. "You think we can hand it back, is that it? Give them a wee apologetic smile?" He looks down and continues shaving. "You have no idea who we're dealing with."

"No shit, which is my point exactly. And at this stage, might I add, there is no *we* since it was *you* who stole it. I need to know everything, man, or I'll just walk out the door right now." I look away momentarily, let him absorb my comment. "And by the way, why do you shave your legs?"

There's a level of resignation in his voice. "There's no turning back."

"What?"

He looks at me with his mad blue eyes – the kind you try to avoid like staring into the sun. "It's all about the clean feel, Kurt. Once you experience it you can never go back." He begins lathering his other leg. "Okay, I may as well tell you what I know."

For a moment, after he's 'fessed up, I'm hesitant to believe anything that has come out of his mouth. Even though most of it seems plausible I have to remind myself it's not like he's a close friend of mine. Sure, we do have *something* in common apart from weed. He rock climbs, and what I know about climbers is they're usually pretty straight up, no hidden agenda. Lincoln is an exception to the rule though – a different breed. In the short time I've got to know him I've reached the conclusion he has no filter, no fear button, no line he won't cross, and when he does cross it he moves with such speed and conviction I sense a kind of perilous energy I love to feed off. So in a way I've had a hand in this, wanted some excitement at least, except now I'm deep over my head, scuba diving, swimming with the sharks.

I pace the room, reflect on what he's told me.

The money, he claims, belongs to a Wellington gang – the Grim Reapers. Who the hell calls themselves that? He says he knows this through a dealer in Auckland who is mates with a grower currently in prison. The grower, not an actual gang member himself, was once contracted by the Reapers to grow Skunk in one of their hothouses. It was when he was working for them that the grower came to know of this bag and its location. He thought that while in the clink, if he told his dealer buddy about it, he could get it lifted, split it two ways without him being suspected. A sweet plan, a sound alibi, except that Lincoln got wind of it.

I stop and turn. "It doesn't make sense. Why on earth would this dealer guy tell you?"

He grins, smoothing moisturiser into his thighs. "Yeah, well, I don't think he intended to. Not when he was boozed off his tits. It wasn't exactly hard to extract the address, although he kept whispering and giggling like a fool, so maybe it was possible I didn't get the full picture." He grins even wider – his teeth are so white they seem to glow out of his face. "I just guessed the bag was full of weed." He slaps his hands together, looks down at the bag. "My God, how much do you think is in there?"

I go over to the window. Below is Cuba Street and the quaint café world is closing down, surrendering to the bar and club scene of Friday night. That sense of anticipation before hitting the clubs, it's hitting me tenfold and I haven't even dropped anything yet. It seems the closer I am to peril the more I come alive.

I turn to face Lincoln. "So, the guy chasing you, you know him?"

He shrugs. "A Reaper, I guess. I know some of the gang, or should I say, they know me from past dealings. But not this guy, thank God, or we'd really be screwed. And don't worry. I'm absolutely positive your face wouldn't even register to him. He's probably some halfwit who wouldn't be able to retain an image of what you or I look like even if he tried."

I should be more sceptical, but I'm inclined to think he's right. It happened so fast the guy probably didn't get a visual on who else was in the car. "So, if this guy was so dim, how did he almost catch you?"

"Luck," he says. "Pure coincidence. I scoped the house out. Looked empty. The mistake I made was unzipping the bag when I found it. I should've left then, but stared goggle eyed at the prize. It made me sloppy. I walked right out the front door like I owned the place and met *you know who* walking up the path."

"Yeah," I say, tersely. "You almost got me killed. When were you thinking of telling me about your plan, when I was lying in a pool of blood?"

He shrugs. "Who cares, man. We're rich now. We should count it, see how rich we are exactly."

I flinch at his comment. The fact he said 'we' and 'rich' in the same sentence softens the blow of what I had already suspected. He just doesn't usually factor in anybody else when he makes plans. "So, you're sure about this? I mean, what are the chances they're on to us, and what about the car? That guy might have recorded the number plate."

"Relax, man. First of all, that dumb arse hasn't a clue who we are, let alone be able to summon enough brain power to remember a number plate. These guys are halfwits. We've already got the edge on them, man. They're back pedalling, spinning in a panic right now. Don't worry about it."

I shake my head. "I don't know, man. I mean, there's a lot riding on this thing."

"Well don't do anything rash, at least count the Goddamn money already. See what we're riding." He unzips the bag and flips the contents. Bundles of rolls and folded wads actually land with a scattering of thumps on the carpet. There's weight to this pile. Amazing to think cash could have weight in kilos.

I pick up a bundle, then another. "Where do you reckon this money came from, drugs?"

Lincoln nods with an analytical gleam in his eye. "Highly likely, and see how all these bills look – mainly crinkled and beaten up on the edges. I'd say they've been scrunched in a hurry, pushed down someone's pocket or folded in the palm of a hand." He pauses to deliberate. "What you see here is the sum of a thousand drug transactions, maybe more."

"Geez, I didn't think patched members hustled the streets. Wouldn't they stand out a little? I thought they would only deal in large amounts."

He looks at me as if I'm stupid. "They do. But then they hire minions to do their dirty work. If a minion gets caught by the pigs, do you think they would squeal? He'd be a right imbecile to mention a syllable that would lead back to the gang. He would be signing his death warrant."

I swallow hard. "Oh, I see."

We separate the cash into two piles and spend the next half hour counting. At the end we disclose our totals. "I'd say about a quarter in mine," Lincoln says.

"A quarter what?"

"Do I have spell it out? *One* quarter *of one* million."

I look down at my own pile. "I've got about the same. So, that's... that's..."

Lincoln grins confidently. "A sweet half-mil right there, and it's all ours." He pauses to catch my eye. "You know, if you stick with me, see this through, half will be yours."

"You're taking the piss, right? I mean, you masterminded this whole thing."

"Sure," he says. "Although you did get shot at, and for that I think you may have an earned a place in the stakes. And besides, I need you in on this."

"For what, I thought you said this was pretty straightforward, no dramas?"

"Yeah I did. But if, and I'm meaning a low chance here, things were to go another way."

"And what way would that be, Lincoln?" I stand and return to the window. "Christ, man. I thought you were certain this was all good?"

"Yes, it is good. How can it not be? Look at it. There's just that one percent chance they find out it was me. Then we're going to have to switch to plan B. That's when you come in. You're an anonymous face who can mobilise the cash right under their noses. You're the X factor, Kurt. The back-up if it all goes pear-shaped."

All the anxiety, all the usual fear that should accompany my decision is blocked, not just by a small handout, but by the kind of money that could set me up a sweet lifestyle dream. I could pay off my student loan, chase a never-ending summer around the globe. This is more than just a free ticket – this is an escape pod from the tyranny of the ordinary. And it's the ordinary I fear most. "So, you're saying this option B is highly unlikely, right?"

He nods, stares intensely. "I'm not playing you, man. If you follow my plan, in a couple of days this will all be over and we'll split this puppy down the middle, go our separate ways. I promise you."

I'm wary of a line I'm about to cross. This might be the second mistake I've made in the last twenty-four hours, but to turn back now would be too safe, too pedestrian – the very skin I'm trying to shed.

I lift my hand to shake on it. "Fifty-fifty then."

He grips firmly, smiles. "Now, how about we break out some of that hard-earned cash?"

3

I have little to compare this to. The last time I stole something I was fourteen. My friend and I broke into the bar of our local tennis club. We concocted a tool out of barbeque tongs which we slid through the roll cage to tap open the till. We pinched a stack of fivers. For the first time in my life this warm crazy rush filled my pubescent brain. I remember pedalling home on a new adrenaline high with a world full of possibility. It was a strange lesson to learn, I guess. Sometimes you could actually get away with this stuff, and what's more be rewarded for it.

I'm having that same feeling now except the stakes are a lot higher and the money stolen is not exactly taken from the mouths of babes. The 'crime part' kind of cancels out when you steal from a criminal organisation. Nevertheless, the consequences of being caught by this gang would make prison seem like a holiday health spa. It does seem a tad premature, though, being in public so soon and with the money left stashed under the bed. Lincoln reassured me that if the gang were on to us, it would make zero difference. In fact, he argued it would be safer being amongst a crowd than cooped up in room, waiting for the door to be smashed down. I kinda see his point. I just can't help thinking someone's watching. Lincoln doesn't seem bothered at all.

We start on Cuba Street, sink a couple of pints, then onto Hummingbird where Lincoln orders pretty much everything on the menu, especially the most expensive items, along with a three-hundred-dollar bottle of Dom Perignon. "I thought this was going to be a quiet night?" I say, taking a swill of Champagne only to spill five dollars-worth on my shirt.

Lincoln starts cutting into a piece of eye fillet. "Fuck, man. You don't get it." He shoves the meat into his mouth, begins to chew aggressively, but keeps talking. "It doesn't matter if we returned all the money tonight. They'll still want our heads on a stick, regardless. May as well spend some of the cash while we can."

"Or what," I say. "Tomorrow when they come with their sticks?" I drain the flute and pour another to the brim. "So," I ask. "What's this plan anyhow? Do we just sit and wait, or should we like, split, take off to the South Island, you know, just in case? And the other thing, perhaps we should get rid of the car, trade it in. There's probably not too many green Toyota Starlets around with smashed windows."

Lincoln's not even looking at me when I'm saying this. His mouth has stopped chewing. His eyes are on a waitress across the room with thin blonde dreads tied back.

"Lincoln, I want you to be serious for a moment."

He fires me a glance. "Serious about what?"

"About this plan you've got?"

He sighs, puts his fork down. "Look, man, can't we just enjoy ourselves tonight?" He looks around at the restaurant, grinning. "See all these folks – this is what true fear looks like – people sipping their pinot noir, hiding behind their safe nine to five jobs they do so well." He leans closer, looks at me directly. "Can you hear that sound?"

"Hear what?"

"That's the daily grind of people marching to the orders of mediocrity. It's everywhere, man. They can't sleep unless they're sure they won't default on their mortgage. They're slaves to the wage, Kurt. Slaves to debt. We don't have to work. For once in our lives we don't have to worry where the next dollar comes from." He turns and signals the waitress for another bottle.

He's right. How many times had I watched my father drag himself off to work – his face filled with about as much enthusiasm as the walking dead. Dad lived for the weekend. That's three quarters of his life sacrificed for a slither of contentment. There is no doubt this is where I want to be, sitting on this edge, looking down at my hands visibly shaking – perhaps a sure sign the shackles are off.

The waitress returns holding the Dom P out front for us to verify, about to pour a sampler. "Oh, don't worry about that," says Lincoln, "I'm sure it's fine." She places the bottle between us, tucks a loose blonde dread behind her ear. "Everything all right with your meal?"

Lincoln looks up and says with a casual, confident air, "Couldn't be better. How's your night going?"

She blushes a little. "It's going okay, I guess."

"But I take it you'd rather be somewhere else?"

She looks away trying to hide a smile. "Yeah, maybe."

"I'm Lincoln, by the way," he says. "And this is Kurt."

While they engage in small talk, it occurs to me that Lincoln is ignoring the fact she is at work. The waitress is certainly showing all the signs she's attracted to him – direct eye contact, relaxed posture, pretending she's got all the time in the world to chat. Certainly not coming up with excuses to leave. Sure, he's an attractive guy which must add to his charm – not only his perfect white teeth and surf boy tan to accentuate his smile, but a strong jaw line to mark his masculinity with a capital M. But it's more than that. It's his unrestrained confidence that draws them in – his ability to charm without trying. I wouldn't mind a piece of what he's got. It would be the perfect antidote to my shy retarded state when it comes to women. Looking at her now, she's got that whole 'alternative thing' going on – cutesy nose stud, ocean blue eyes, and when she smiles these dimples appear that could warm the cold in anyone's heart.

"Nice to meet you guys," she says. "I'm Helen, by the way." She picks up the empty bottle. "You celebrating something important tonight?"

"Yeah. The quest for unemployment," Lincoln says.

She frowns a little.

"You know, taking a few months off, traveling around and stuff. You got anything planned this summer?"

26

She sighs. "If the stars align, I might get to Takaka for The Gathering this new year's."

"Hey, I've heard great things about that rave. Perhaps I can help you out with the stars?"

She pauses with a half-formed smile, unsure as to how to respond.

"I mean, we're probably heading over there at some stage, if you want a ride. No strings attached. If you have friend, boyfriend, whatever, you're welcome to bring them along."

She nods. "Generous offer… but you know, I have no fixed plans as yet."

"Oh well, the offer stands," he says. "And one other thing, you might be able to help us. We're practically tourists. You know of any good bars in town?"

"Yeah, there's one place worthwhile. You know Mighty Mighty on Cuba?"

He nods. "I think we passed it earlier."

"Well, you should check it out later. My friend's playing there tonight. I'm heading there after work."

"Sure, sounds good, I'll consider it," he says, and, without an iota of desperation in his voice he adds, "Might see you in Mighty Mighty." He smiles and the waitress walks off with a distinct lightness in her step.

I turn to him. "You're unbelievable."

He pours the Champagne, "What do you mean?"

"You know, your whole James Bond routine?"

He grins, shrugs. "I was just being friendly."

After paying the exorbitant bill we sample a series of bars that disappoint, but we soldier on in hope of greener pastures. I'm too drunk to care, let alone able to tame Lincoln into a minute of his attention to the critical situation we're in. I need to drink at his pace just to keep up this level of apathy towards our impending doom. I'm surviving on an apocalyptic perspective – everything is going to end, soon, may as well live it up while we can.

This is all going swimmingly until Lincoln tells me a story about how he kissed a guy once. "You know how it is," he says. "I just wanted to make sure I wasn't missing out. Have you ever wondered what it's like? I thought maybe I could just try it once? But I couldn't get past the stubble. It was like kissing sandpaper." He takes a sip of whisky. "Man, it's really in our genes what aligns our sexual nature." He turns to me. "So, Kurt, you ever…"

"Been with a guy?" I shake my head, mumble something under my breath.

He interjects suddenly. "What did you say?"

I take a solid mouthful of Glenfiddich, annoyed at myself. But this situation I'm in has unlocked a certain honesty box inside my brain and I'm not sure what else is going to come out. "I said I haven't even been with anyone."

"No way, you're eating my arsehole. You're a virgin!" he says, really loudly, but I really don't care.

"Yes, Lincoln, that I am!" I gulp the rest of the scotch and signal the bartender for another. I look over at him and he's still smiling.

"It's not that funny," I say.

"Sorry, I mean, you're seriously telling me you've never done it?"

I shake my head.

"Why?" he asks. "What's stopped you?"

I shrug. "I could tell you my list of close encounters, however, every time an opportunity presents itself booze seems to get in the way. But I guess you don't really want. to hear about that."

He grins. "You mean you get limp dick?"

"Worse," I say.

He leans in. "You want some advice?"

"Sure, what have I got to lose?"

"All they really want is for you to go up and talk to them. And when I mean talk, make them feel like you're really listening. If you don't give them any attention at all then they'll think you're not interested." He pauses. "I'm guessing you're the shy type who doesn't show them any attention, you're too chicken shit. Am I right?"

I nod. Believe it or not, he's struck a chord. When it comes to the opposite sex, I have a retard switch in my brain. By the time I've gathered enough courage to talk to them I would've drunk enough booze to anaesthetise a mad Russian. Any hope of courting is usually stamped out by the horrid lurching movements in my approach, my slurring tongue and a crazed look in my eyes that tells them in no uncertain terms, *run.* Where did I get this hopeless disposition? I have no problems climbing a fifty-metre cliff, so why then the Chernobyl meltdown when it comes to women?

Lincoln scopes the bar, and when he looks at me again I'm expecting he's spotted some girl I should approach as a kind of test. "Come to think of it," he says, "what you need is to just get it over with." He punches me lightly in the arm. "You must be bursting at the seams, man. The worst case of blue balls, I bet. If you go out there right now you're likely going to screw it up and come across desperate. You'll either be slapped or beaten up or something." He rubs his hands together, grins. "I think tonight I've got just the plan."

"That wouldn't be '*the* plan' about tomorrow, would it? About the wee gang problem we've got on our hands?"

"Fuck tomorrow." He orders a fresh row of tequilas. We throw them back.

4

In front of us are nine women lined up for inspection. All of them Asian, dolled up in tight miniskirts with mouths thick with lipstick. We've found our way up to this place via a thin row of stairs from the street and a neon sign flashing *Massage*. No points for originality. I really believed that perhaps all that was going on in these kinds of places was just that. When Lincoln approached the reception, a lady with a tired, cancerous face asked if we wanted a massage or 'the full service'. Lincoln assured her we were here for the latter. The lady escorted us through a secure door and now I'm standing in front of these nine stony faces already bored by the selection process. I've been standing here for a while, in limbo of what to do. The lady glances at her watch, looks up. "You choosing or not? I've got customers waiting."

Lincoln's already hinted at the one on the left who I'm sure is slightly taller than I am although that's not really the issue. They all seem all right, it's just this place and me (the customer) picking out a leg of ham from the frozen section. How has my university education prepared me for this? Camus would say life is a cycle of mundane actions; get out of bed, brush your teeth, go to work… etcetera. But this is anything but mundane. Sartre, on the other hand, would be lecturing me on responsibility for my actions – what am I really committing myself to? This is huge for me. Anxiety, frigidity, ambivalence permeate my very core, yet Lincoln seems right at home, nudging me to hurry up. "Come on, man. Just pick."

At that moment one of them smiles; whether this means she actually has an infinitesimal amount of attraction towards me or not is enough to make this transaction seem just a tad more human. I point my finger. "That one," I say, timidly.

"Candy," the lady says, "you go with him, one hour." The girl approaches and takes my hand gently, smiles. I'm sure her name is not Candy, likely a long unpronounceable name with a real history, a real family. I can envision her aunts and uncles, her parents watching me from a gallery high up, their arms folded and their eyes filled with the kind of cold reserved for perpetrators. She continues to smile. "Come," she says.

I turn to Lincoln, expecting he's going to pick as well. "See you later," he says, waving me off.

"Wait. This was your idea."

He shakes his head disapprovingly. "This is not my style." He grins and turns to leave.

"Where are you going?"

"I've got a date, remember. With that waitress, Helen."

I'm in the shower. I presumed we were going to get straight to it. I didn't understand her at first, she just kept pointing at the glass shower box as I stood naked in front of her. I thought maybe she wanted to do it in the shower standing up until she led me in by the hand. "You. In there. Clean first, yes."

So, I turn out to be a very smelly customer, which figures since I haven't washed in twenty-four hours and have been sweating ever since I left Auckland. It actually feels good under a steady flow of hot water, relaxed even. Through the glass I can make out Candy preparing the king size bed with towels, box of tissues, condoms and lubricant, and then she starts stripping off herself. I wipe away the condensation to get a better look. She's slight, like most Asians are. I put her age at mid-twenties. My dick springs to life as if watching porn through the glass, not registering that this is real – a real person I'm about to fornicate with.

I get out and towel off, nervous now – my so-called erection deflating to a small cheerio. Candy flops onto the bed and lies to her side, staring straight at my genitalia. "Oh, so big," she says, beckoning me to sit beside her. This is clearly a lie. I've never been big. I never will be big. My appendage, I believe, having conducted a series of measurements, is just below average, I think. Not small, I don't think I could be in the small category. Just a tiny bit below average.

I sit on the edge of the bed, my back to her. Of all the images that could be flowing through my head, I picture my mother – a slow but horrified look on her face with the protest of a thousand feminist voices, chanting *Don't do it*. She touches me, rubs her hand over my shoulders, down my spine. "You want massage. Lie down." I do as I'm told and feel oil dripped onto my back and her strong wiry hands kneading my shoulders and slowly down to my buttocks. "Turn over," she instructs. Flipping onto my back, I peer down at my cock flopped to its side like a dead sardine. How many of these has she seen in her career? A whole dead ocean filled with lifeless sea urchins longing to be touched. I'm filled with a pathetic loathing for my phallic member. Hopeless, but nevertheless Candy gets to work, prying open a condom and rolling it on with some difficulty before commencing with a hand job. She grips and shakes the thing senseless. With all her professional might she could be stretching and contracting a soft marshmallow. I close my eyes and think erection thoughts. This is embarrassing, nothing comes. It all feels cold and numb down there. She stops. "Ah, you drink too much. Too drunk."

"No," I plead. "Just wait, I'll be all right in a second."

"Okay," and she keeps prodding on, changing hands to give her other hand a rest. Then after a while she stops and I'm thinking it's all over until I hear an electric buzzing sound. I look up and she's got a nine-inch vibrating dildo gripped in her hand. I momentarily clench my butt cheeks. "What is that for?"

"You want? It make you horny. I try, yes. Just a little bit of rub on your arse" She barely starts towards me with that thing and I spring to my feet.

"No," I say. "Me don't want that." She stands holding the member in front of her, whirring like a weapon. I notice that the actual head on the thing is rotating. This is a sure sign that any notion of sex will now involve this apparatus. "You can put that away," I tell her, pulling on my pants.

"You have time left," she says.

"Keep it. Thanks for everything, truly."

She's got that look like she's offering a freebie of some kind. I turn and take off down the stairs, out into the street, my long wet hair clinging after me.

5

One problem has resolved itself when I wake in the backpackers the next morning. That is, any future desire to visit a brothel is extinguished on the basis of last night. I'd rather ice curl butt naked while lip syncing to Milli Vanilli than revisit that again. This leaves the bigger, more ominous problem underneath the bed – half a million reasons for a gang to hunt us down and inflict grievous bodily harm.

It's already late morning but I can't will my body to stand. I have the Sahara Desert in my mouth and some tiny man in my brain hammering nails when I try to move. I manage to tilt my head and see two bodies lumped in each other's arms on the bed adjacent. Lincoln is easily identified – he's lying supine, comatose with one arm underneath this chick, whose face is practically buried in his armpit. She's got thin blonde dreads splayed out on the pillow. God, I hope it's not her. Normally I wouldn't be bothered, but given the situation the last thing we need is to get her involved.

Bearing the pain, I sit up, feel the blood re-balancing in the chambers of my skull before I stumble across the room to wake the shit out of Lincoln. As I get closer, the girl stirs, turning her face. Identity confirmed – the waitress, Helen. She flicks her arm to clear away some of the sheet, exposing her breasts. Her eyes remain closed. Oh man, I shouldn't be looking but they do lighten the hangover. That is until I notice Lincoln grinning up at me.

"Hey, stop perving!"

Helen wakes, sits up, a little startled, wraps the sheet around her when she notices me standing there. "Hi," she says, shyly. "I didn't know... um... you were..."

I fill her in to relieve some embarrassment. "Don't worry, you must have been already asleep when I came in last night."

"Oh." She squints up at me. "I forgot your name."

"Kurt."

She yawns, "Oh yeah... that's right."

The conversation practically dies right there. Even though I'm sure her yawn was genuine, I can't help thinking that compared to Lincoln I must be like background noise – unremarkable, somewhat beige.

Lincoln breaks the silence, behaving like everything is tickety-boo. "Man, I'm hungry. We should get a bite to eat. Brunch," he proposes.

I'm assuming he is meaning all of us, including her which disturbs me. "Lincoln, I think we need to talk."

"Shoot," he says, stretching. "What do you want to talk about?"

"Well. How can I put this? Last night I didn't sleep so well, I had this nightmare that there was something underneath my bed, haunting me."

He nods, like he gets it. "I'd say you need a shrink."

Helen smiles, and now I'm starting to wonder whether she knows about the money? Surely Lincoln can't be that stupid. Maybe I'm the stupid one. I don't feel a jot of confidence about this scene.

"Relax, dude," Lincoln says, probably noticing that I've gone pale. "Sure, I'll have a chat."

We leave her in the room and stand in the hallway in just our underwear. "What the fuck, man," I whisper. "You'd better get rid of her soon."

He shrugs. "Why? I like her."

"Hey, we can't drag her into this. We've got some serious business to sort out."

He looks at me and says one word. "Manual."

"Huh?"

"She drives a manual, doofus. I tried to arrange an automatic, but—"

"What the hell are you talking about?"

"I've already sold the car. While you were sleeping I snuck out of bed, did a sweet deal with an Israeli tourist. Sold it to him for a dollar and he took it off my hands no questions asked, except for one condition – that he drive it away this morning."

"Great," I say, feeling some confidence restored. "But what has that got to do with her being able to drive manual?"

He doesn't answer, looks surprisingly bright eyed and nervous all of a sudden as we hear someone stomping down the hall. An inconsequential backpacker passes by.

Lincoln points towards the male toilet, drags me in there and locks the door behind us.

"Hey, what's this about?"

"Relax," he says. "It's just better this way, trust me."

"Why, it's not like the gang is on to us. I mean, like you said, there's nothing to worry about, right?"

He looks down. "Yeah, well. That was yesterday. There's been an update."

"You're fucking with me, is that it?" I stare at him, he makes direct eye contact, and now I'm terrified of what he's about to say.

"Last night I noticed someone following us."

"What the fuck do you mean, us?"

"I mean, it was me they were following. While you were getting down busy in that brothel, I was being watched. I've seen this guy before – Kane 'rip you a new arsehole' Mason, a real psycho who gets the job done."

"What kind of job?"

"He's a Reaper, dip shit. What do you think he does, accountancy? He hunts people down, gets whatever is owing. In other words we're now on his hit list."

Again he refers to 'us' and it unnerves me. "You mean he is after you, right? Please tell me I'm not known yet."

"Relax, man. You haven't been identified."

I breathe a sigh of relief and at the same time relieve my bladder onto the porcelain bowl with an urgent flow.

Lincoln continues. "What this means, of course, is that Kane might be waiting for me out on the street, probably him and some others. I can't risk going out there."

I miss, splatter the floor. "I'm pleased you're finally filling me in." I shake the drips and flush. "So, when are we going for brunch? I think I like that idea best."

"Fuck, man. The reason why I suggested brunch is I don't want her to get anxious and shit. Just act normal around her, I don't want her to suspect anything out of the ordinary. What I want is for you to go with her, they won't know you guys. Stuff the money in your pack. If they catch sight of the blue bag you're history. Kane is not the kind of guy you want to meet."

I smile, but more out of a coping mechanism to deal with the crazy shit I'm hearing. Now I'd rather lip sync to Milli Vanilli while Candy inserts a dildo up my ass. "Wait a minute. Yesterday you were saying there were no dramas. Now you've got the gang waiting for you outside, those 'half-wits' I think you called them. They are probably not that dumb, huh? So, how I see it, you can stick the money. I'd rather be poor than beaten to death."

I try to leave but he grabs me by the shoulders. "But what's the risk? All you have to do is take the money, and if something should happen to me it's all yours anyway. They haven't a clue who you are. They'll think you are just a couple of tourists leaving the hostel."

I pause to consider. Despite what Lincoln is telling me the risk is the same. I have to leave the building at some stage, with or without the money. His logic has a disturbing clarity. But what's more disturbing is perhaps an unconscious part of me knew this would probably happen but went along with it anyway.

"All right, I'll consider it, but what then?"

He lets go, relaxes a little. "I've arranged for you to pick up a car. A getaway car if you like, but this ain't no bat-mobile. Quite the opposite. I've scheduled for you to meet the seller in Aro Valley, in an hour. You think you could do that?"

"Do what exactly?"

"Buy the car and meet me back here. I'm going to try and exit the rear of the building, on Victoria Street. They're unlikely to be monitoring that part."

I pause for a moment. "Exiting the rear sounds too risky. How about abseiling out the window? We'll take your pack and leave you with the rope and harness. From memory, I'm pretty sure our room is positioned perfectly above a secluded alley. They won't expect that."

He smiles, pats me on the back. "Now you're getting into the swing of things, man. I like that idea."

6

As Helen and I slip out the front door I can sense the skin of my mortality. It has never been this intimate. Before it has only been an idea, like a theory yet to be proved. All the data is in, my nerve endings are exploring new pathways of impending terror.

No one comes at us with a machete. Not even the slightest sign of being followed. The claws retract a little, just enough to breathe in the sun and the fresh southerly toying with my hair. A warm wave of unspent adrenaline washes over me, and this feeling is incomparable to anything else, enriching the senses, making me mindful of my breath and the simplicity of stepping one foot in front of the other. For a moment life makes perfect sense. Just keep breathing, moving, it's all I really need to do. There is really nothing to worry about. Helen thinks all we're doing is buying a car for a road trip (a trip she's been invited on) while Lincoln has to attend to 'other business'.

Halfway up Aro Valley the confidence starts to wear thin. Something feels fundamentally odd. It's not that I'm carrying half a million on my back, or that Lincoln is probably curled up, paranoid, waiting for our return, or that all this could go horribly pear-shaped. No, it's none of that, even though each would equally qualify. It's her motive. Helen could have anyone she wanted, and yet she is willing, on a whim, to give up her job and instil so much trust in Lincoln. It beckons me to ask, "So, I guess you've had to quit your job. Don't you think that's a bit drastic? I mean, you've only just met."

She smiles. "Why, is there something I should know about him?"

I bite my tongue. I should tell her. Any decent person would let her know what she's really getting into, but I can't. At the very least I could dissuade her a little without disclosing any detail. "Well, he's a bit different, I guess. Not the average kind of guy. When you're with him you never really know what's around the corner. He's pretty erratic and spontaneous most of the time."

"And you don't like that about him?"

I shake my head. "The opposite. He's unlike any person I know. He seems to run on a different set of rules. Or more pointedly, no rules whatsoever."

She turns to me, grins. "And so, you think, just because I'm a girl I'd be put off by that?"

I pause, stutter my words. "Um... I didn't mean to... ah..."

She smiles. "Oh, I get it?"

Even though I sense she's toying with me a little, I could easily forgive her for that smile of hers. We walk in silence a little way, before she glances over at me. "So, Kurt, I hope you don't mind me saying, but you don't seem the type of guy who hangs around someone like Lincoln."

43

"Really," I reply. "How did you come to that conclusion? You barely know me."

"Exactly," she says.

I grin to myself. "Okay. Point taken."

"And besides I already know about what you're trying to say."

"You do?"

"About the money thing. I know all about it." She pauses. "You know, it's what I'd do if I was given an early inheritance. Real sad about his parents though." She sighs. "Must feel lonely now that he's got no family left. If I was him, I'd be doing exactly this, blowing some... just for the hell of it."

I swallow hard, my mouth dries up. "Um... yeah... I agree."

"I mean, don't think I'm just coming along because of his money. I told him I wasn't a charity case, but he insisted, told me he'd be sadder than ever if I didn't come along. There was no way I could turn him down, not after what he'd been through, must've been totally devastating."

I breathe a sigh of relief. "Yeah... totally."

"And besides, how can I turn down a road trip to working all summer on a crappy wage?"

I stare at the traffic going past. "I guess I have to agree with you on that one. My biggest fear is getting a steady job. Next to losing my parents, I'd say that would be the most tragic of all."

"That's taking it a bit too far, don't you think?"

I look at her. "I'm being serious. It totally petrifies me. The idea of wasting the best years of your life in some fat profit margin of some company. Now that's tragic. That's like, you died before you even started breathing. There's no way I'm heading into that trap."

Helen shrugs. "I know what you mean, but at some point we're going to have to cave in for a proper job. My student loan isn't getting any smaller."

"How big is it?"

She pauses. "How big is yours?"

"Oh, mine's pretty hefty."

"Well, I'm pretty sure mine is in the stratosphere thanks to changing my major."

"What did you end up with?"

"It was classics to begin with then anthropology, but you know, neither of those are going lead to paid employment. So, I've finished with English Lit. At least that way I can go to teachers' college."

I smile. "So that's what you want to be, an English teacher?"

"Yeah, I think so?"

"You don't sound convinced."

"Well, it's a job I wouldn't mind so much. It would pay the bills, give me enough to travel and stuff." She looks across at me. "What about you, what's your plan?"

I sigh. "Well, with a BA in philosophy I guess I'll be getting a job at McDonald's." I give her a cheesy grin. "Would you like fries with that?"

"Yeah," she says, playing along, "and I'd like to upsize everything, forever, until I'm one gigantic ball of lard."

"Great. Can't wait to assist."

"No but really, what's your plan?"

I hesitate, sensing the natural urge to spill the beans. So far, I've probably sustained the longest conversation with a member of the female species without being off my tits. This is a personal best.

I shrug. "This is it. Beyond this I haven't much going on." *God, now I sound like a no-hoper.* "I mean, I'm not quite sure yet. Just keeping my options open and stuff."

She pauses to reflect. "Nice way to be if you can afford it. I guess I'm just sick of being dirt poor all the time. I want to travel, see the world."

I have a brief mad thought – somewhere in a parallel universe we are having this exact conversation, except she never meets Lincoln and the money I'm carrying is actually clean, and we book the next plane out of here.

7

The car Lincoln has arranged is a red 1982 Skoda. I've checked the address twice. I don't get it, why this piece of crap? But who cares, really. The guy wants a thousand bucks, so I shell out that exact amount in stolen one hundred dollar bills. I can smell the guy's desperation. He's just another broke-arse student, like most of us – up to our eyeballs in student debt. He takes the money eagerly and points to where I need to sign on the change of ownership papers.

"Wait a minute," Helen asks. "Aren't you going to test drive it first, or at least bargain him down a little?"

The guy butts in before I can answer. "It's a good car. European, you know. Worth every penny."

Helen picks up the papers and studies them carefully. "You've got the wrong forms. These are for heavy vehicles, for truck drivers. You can't sign these."

The guy checks them over himself, sighs disappointedly. "I thought I had the right ones."

There's a buyer/seller awkwardness, no one says anything. "Well," I say finally, "I need to buy a car. I've handed over the cash. So, give us the keys and we'll be off."

The guy hands over the keys happily. Helen shakes her head. "What about the ownership papers?"

"Don't worry," I tell her. "We'll pick them up on the way, do it ourselves." I turn to the guy. "If that's all right with you?"

He smiles. "Not a problem."

I slide into the passenger seat and give Helen the keys. "What are you doing?" she asks. "Don't you want to drive?"

I shrug, anticipating the sense of a distinct lack of manliness. "I don't have a license. I don't even know how to drive manual."

8

"So, this is where he said to wait?" Helen asks.

I nod. "Yeah, I think so."

Ten minutes go by, then twenty. I'm scanning the roof line, the alley, along the street. No sign of him anywhere. An image of Kane Mason creeps into my psyche, what I imagine him to be – prison tats covering his entire face so as to block out all natural skin. I look over my shoulder, start to get the fear.

"Why are you so nervous all of sudden?"

I tell a lie. "We've got to catch the Interislander. You know, we've got tickets for the midday sailing."

Helen frowns. "He said nothing about leaving today. I've got to go home and pack."

"Yeah. Well, you can see why I'm nervous then."

"He's probably waiting out front. We should head around there."

I consider this option. I'm sure even if they were waiting outside they still wouldn't know who we were. I agree to check it out.

Helen drops me by the main entrance in the five-minute waiting zone. I ask her to hang in the car. There's still no sign of anyone lurking, so I head straight in making a beeline upstairs to the bedroom. The door's ajar. Perhaps the cleaner's busy in there or Lincoln's flown already? I take a deep breath, nudge the door.

9

I'm trying to keep it together when I get back into the car. Any attempt to talk right now would expose the scared little man inside my head. Helen keeps saying how pale I look, keeps asking what's wrong. That little man is speaking fast paranoid gibberish inside my brain, how it's turning bad, how this time I really fucked up, but I'm able to gag and shackle him. "I think we should just drive on," I tell her, looking over my shoulder.

"Where's Lincoln?"

"He's not in there. I don't know where he is."

"What do you mean?"

"Please, we can't park here, just drive on."

"All right," she says. "Whatever."

She drives along Lambton Quay, to the end and pulls over, cuts the engine. "Now. Can you tell me what's going on?"

I have seconds to come up with something good – a story that is believable. But all that comes is the flashback of an empty room ripped through by a tornado – overturned mattresses, slashed pillows, climbing rope strewn on the floor – a scene of violent interrogation, a scene that has my future scrawled in blood. Perhaps I should just grab my gear and leave, that would be easier, only that she's placed her hand on my shoulder. "Just tell me what's going on, I want to know, otherwise I'm not driving any further."

I don't think I could even explain it to myself. Nothing makes sense anymore. Looking out the window at the busy street of shoppers I'm starting to envy their lives. Perhaps having a regular job and a regular life where your future is predictably laid out is the way to go. It seems to be a lot better than being in this hot seat. "It's hard to explain," I say. I'm considering telling her everything, she deserves to know, but then telling her could make her complicit, potentially put her in harm's way, and that's the last thing I want. "So, you want to know what's going on," I clarify, giving me a moment to think.

She nods.

"Okay then, but you won't believe me when I tell you."

"Tell me already."

"Lincoln… he's, well, from what I can tell of the situation he's gone AWOL."

She frowns. "AWOL, huh?"

"I'm serious. All I know is, Lincoln can flip at any moment. Sometimes he just disappears." I lower my voice. "He's got some kind of mental issue."

"Oh," she says. "What, like bipolar or something?"

"Yeah. Something like that, although his psychiatrist is uncertain. A kind of rare form of mental illness – it only comes on briefly. He can appear normal at first, behaves normally, then vanishes sometimes for days, weeks." Then I add, gulping. "He goes on some kind of 'journey', I'm told."

Helen nods and stares at the dashboard. "All right, that's a pretty good piece of bullshit you've just served me. You must've really thought hard about that one, huh?" She sighs, pulls out her cell phone – the latest model that flips open. "I'm going to call him. What's his number?"

"I don't know it by heart," I lie.

"You must have it stored in your cell?"

"What cell? I don't have one." This time I'm telling the truth. For some reason I've built up an aversion to this new cell phone fad.

Helen looks straight into me it seems. "Thing is, Kurt, whatever the reason, I thought we were going to the South Island. He was all excited, seemed so genuine about it. Then this morning, buying the car, well, it seemed like it was really happening."

I nod, sigh. "Yeah, I know. That's why I was so shocked too." I pause. "Tell you what, if you give me your number I'll call you if he turns up."

She's got that perplexed look, uncertain as to what I just told her. She writes her number down on a piece of paper and hands it to me. "I guess there's not much else I can do." She pauses. "What about this car, is this yours or his?"

"It's both of ours, but you may as well hold onto it for now. It's not like I can drive it anyhow."

"You want a lift somewhere?"

I shake my head. "This will do fine." I gather both backpacks, mine and Lincoln's. "Okay, I'll call ya, hopefully soon," I say, and she does a half wave and drives off.

10

I actually don't know where I'm going, other than heading back into town. Paranoia in public is bad enough let alone feeling stink about lying to Helen. I keep making eye contact with strangers passing me by, wondering if it was me staring at them or the other way around. *Perhaps they know something?* I get halfway along Lambton Quay and stop. The Continental Hotel is across the road. Shelter, I'm thinking, a place of refuge to gather my thoughts. I make a beeline straight for it.

I really don't fit the image when I walk through the sliding doors. "Can I help you, sir," the concierge asks. "Are you lost?"

I'm acutely aware of the contrast between me hoarding two packs on my front and back and the plush air-conditioned lounge. Businessmen in suits stop to look up from their lattes. I probably look homeless with all my worldly possessions strapped to my body – truth is, that's an accurate picture. "Do you have a room?" I ask.

The concierge scans me up and down. I'm unshaven and he's probably smelling last night's booze on me. "We don't do backpacker accommodation, sorry."

"Don't worry. I have money. I can pay up front if you wish."

He smiles. "All we need is a credit card, sir." He guides me over to the check-in. I hand him my visa which has less than zero credit and will probably melt the machine if he actually swiped it. Instead, he takes a carbon copy, like that's going to be worth anything. I fill in my details on the form and hand it back to him. "Listen, about room service, are you still doing breakfast?"

He hands me a menu. "What would you like?"

I scan it over. "Eggs Benedict please, and do you have Champagne, you know, the real French stuff?" My God, I'm ordering booze without even knowing it. A subconscious need.

He hands me a wine list. I can't be bothered going through it. "What about Dom Perignon, do you have that?"

He pauses. "Yes, sir. Four hundred dollars a bottle."

I gulp at the price, forgetting I'm flush.

He clears his throat. "We do have cheaper bottles, sir. May I suggest the Lindaur, it's on special this week."

I pull out a roll, pick off eight hundred and lay it on the counter. "I'll take two bottles." The man eyes the money, not sure what he's seeing, then eventually gathers it up discreetly. "This will go with your deposit, if you don't mind. We usually do the billing at the end."

"Not a problem," I say.

"How many glasses?"

"Huh?"

"For the Champagne, sir."

I pause a moment, better not convey I'm a lonely drunk. "Two glasses, please."

He hands me a key with a small idiot proof map to navigate to my room. "Will you need help with your bags?"

"No thank you."

11

What has taken place in the last twenty-four hours is not entirely clear. I'm still in the hotel room when I wake the following morning. I probably never left. I stay supine, holding back the horror of a ten-tonne hangover that will make its presence known if I try to move. It seems easier to remain still, let the horror seep in slowly. Pulling the sheets over my head dislodges something rolling off the bed. The thud makes me sit up. I rub my eyes and take in the room.

There are a number of empty champagne bottles, miniatures and half eaten plates of food. I've obviously milked the room service thing; a gigantic bill likely awaits downstairs as I try to count the number of Dom Perignon consumed, but it really doesn't matter. I'm doomed anyway. I have done nothing to resolve my situation, not that I think it's resolvable, but getting ripped to shit and going on a bender hasn't improved things.

I hold my head, rock back and forth recounting any saved memories of last night, of yesterday. Pieces come back, nothing I really want to remember: flashes of masturbating to a mindless episode of *Baywatch*; staring countless times out of the high-rise window down on the city lights; masquerading naked around the room with a one hundred dollar bill clenched between my butt cheeks, and yes, pretending to be a girl by shoving my dick between my legs. That kind of stuff. My God, how could I get so fucked up?

I bolt upright. *The money!*

I look under the bed, not there, behind the chaise lounge, under chairs, in the blankets. I check the en suite, cupboards, but nothing. A sickening fear grips me. I check all the places again, emptying my pack, overturning clothes and pillows and flipping the mattress. I slump to the floor, curl into a foetal position, close my eyes. "Fucking shit bag, cunt!" That money is the only thing I've got that could dig me out of this grave. At least if the Reapers show up I could appease them a tad before the knives came out. There are a raft of escape plans I can think of: fleeing the country, going bush, never coming back, or maybe even setting up a deal with the Reapers – they give me Lincoln in exchange for the money kind of gig, but all of these plans require that little pot of gold.

I stand and pace the room, hyperventilating, trying to think where I could have stashed it. Maybe they've come already, been and gone while I was asleep. Lincoln tortured till he squealed my name, perhaps? All they would have to do is guess what an idiot would be up to with the money – locked up in some rich hotel fantasy. But there's no sign of forced entry, and I'm sure I wouldn't have been left unscathed. It *has* to be in here. I continue to pace, racking my brain for ideas, a memory, where the hell did I put it? Nothing comes, I'm all dried up, dehydrated, my body one big throbbing hangover. I reach for the mini bar to get a cool refreshing drink.

Bingo!

My life expectancy has improved somewhat since I found the bag. Why I stuffed it in there I don't know, but not a bad hiding place considering, so I left it there and closed the fridge door.

I'm down in the foyer, checking emails. Or pretending to do so anyhow as I troll the internet for anything I can dig up on the Reapers. This is the result of spending the morning in deep paranoia. What I've worked out is that most plans I can think of end badly. If I run away then they will follow. I could go overseas, never come back, but if they know who I am then they'll get to my family. Fleeing would mean permanent extradition, division of the soul. I couldn't handle that. Lincoln may or may not have told them about me yet. It's been twenty-four hours. At some point I'm sure he'll crack. The longer I leave it the more chance he'll squeal, if he hasn't already. The other factor is, if I do nothing then I'll have blood on my hands. I'm no deserter. No, this requires extraordinary action in the face of an extraordinary fear. A scouting mission at the very least, or I'm dead or forgotten anyway. Besides, although faced with a formidable task ahead, there is no denying this crazy part of me that's starting to come alive.

The internet comes up with a couple of hits. An article excerpt from a social anthropologist on the history of gangs in New Zealand. There's an old photo inset of the gang in front of a house. It's tagged 'The Grim Reapers in front of their Farley Street Headquarters in Newtown'. I click onto a city map of Wellington. Newtown isn't that far from here. An easy thirty-minute walk.

12

Turns out I've been looking at Tarantino films the wrong way. I also know that something bad is about to happen. There's good evidence to suggest my existence is imminently doomed. For one, I'm sitting next to Lincoln, stripped down to my underwear and tied in the same manner as him – hands bound behind my back, ankles lashed to the chair legs, and if I were to stand I would just keel over as my midsection is strapped down as well. We're looking at each other, gagged, studying the whites of our eyes although I'm certain he's not as terrified as I am, given he hasn't a stream of urine pooling beneath him. In Tarantino films there's always at least one guy who gets graphically tortured, but to such an extent it becomes over the top, almost comically absurd. I'm now that guy and I'm not laughing.

It must be three, maybe four in the morning. The house is quiet. No alarm has been raised. So far there's only been one man running this show. He's kindly introduced himself. We are in the sole custody of his lordship, Kane Mason. My head is throbbing from his king hit. My mouth painfully stretched to accommodate his sock which he pulled fresh off his feet. A little starter, he had said, stuffing it in my gob. On the palate, balsamic vinegar strained through old man's undies comes to mind.

After a wait, Kane enters the basement having nipped out to get 'his gear'. He's carrying what a carpenter might bring to a job – a black toolbox. Death tiptoes silently through me as he unbuckles the lid. He turns a chair around and sits down, leans towards us, doesn't say anything, just smiles. His red afro hair and fair skin have all the hallmarks of an albino freak, and to top it off his eyes, well, there is only one way to describe his eyes – two bleached arseholes staring straight at me.

"So, I see you've joined our little party." He grins, reaches down and pulls out four items from the box: Stanley knife, hammer, pliers, and what I recognise as a nutcracker. He touches each one, as if adoring his little pets, straightens them in a line. There must be an order. I just don't know from which end he'll begin.

He picks up the Stanley, pauses, then puts it down, picks up the nutcracker instead. Something has changed his mind. He gives me another dose of his arsehole eyes. "What happened to my dogs?"

What happened to his dogs is that they got incredibly stoned. I know this because I fed them a whole space cake I found in the bottom of Lincoln's pack. It had enough THC to set my mind ablaze for a month.

As planned, I had scouted the place out in the afternoon. I thought it safe enough to walk by their barred gates. At ten to fifteen minute intervals I walked by taking snapshot observations. First, I noticed the unchained dogs

– they weren't hard to miss, gnashing their grizzly Rottweiler teeth. Then I took note of the entrance to the house, followed by a side entrance that seemed to be descending into some kind of basement. The green fence at the rear was the weakness and easily accessed through their neighbour's property. I had no real intention at this point of actually breaking in but then on the last sneak by there was someone coming up from the basement. He didn't notice me. My eyes were quick but I was one hundred percent certain he was carrying Lincoln's harness. A red and grey Petzl with a climbing sling dangling from it. So that's where they were keeping him, I thought. All I had to do was take care of the dogs and pick a time when they were all asleep.

I try to speak. "Hmmm... mmmm... hmmm... mmmmm..." I'm trying to tell him where the money is, straight off. No games. If he just loosened the gag a little he'd have what he wanted, instantly.

"I said, what happened to my dogs? Can't you talk, boy?" He scrapes the chair closer so that he's at arm's length, running the nutcracker slowly up my thigh, stopping just short of the crotch. "I know what you want to say. You want to tell me where the money is, right?" I nod, emphatically. Lincoln makes a muffled sound, straining in his chair. Kane turns with a slow menacing glance. "Shut the fuck up." Lincoln goes quiet. The cold steel of the nutcracker maintains its contact. He returns his eyes on me.

"Thing is, boy, you can tell me everything now, or you could tell me later. It won't make a shit of difference." He smiles a set of nicotine-stained teeth. "You might be wondering why I haven't woken the others yet. To tell you the truth, it would be sad to miss out on some fun. You see, I enjoy this. It's my profession." He glides his hand over his tools. "It would be a shame not to keep up my practising hours, eh?"

I'm nodding, not sure what I'm nodding to, perhaps torture, yes, I think I'm consenting to torture.

He grits his teeth. "So, what happened to my dogs? Did you bloody poison them, did ya? You randy fucker." He grabs the Stanley knife, severs the elastic band of my undies and rips them off violently. "You want this, don't you?" I'm squirming, trying to shield my privates, but there's nothing I can do. If they could shrivel up and hide right now I would give them full permission. He puts his hand around my neck, squeezes. "Calm the fuck down." I freeze, his grip releases a little. I can feel the cold steel cupping my testicles. He leans right up close, breathes on me. "Do you like spaghetti and meatballs, boy?"

I nod, quickly.

"I had spaghetti and meatballs last night. The leftovers I gave to the dogs, but the thing is, they didn't get any *meat...balls*." He squeezes the tool a little firmer. "Don't you think that would be a shame, if they were to go without?" I nod and continue to nod for no reason than to slow the inevitable. "Let's count to three, shall we, ready... One!"

I hold my breath, begin to pray. *God, if you can hear me,* now *is the time to intervene.*

"Two!"

I close my eyes, regret everything.

The mistake I made was to assume no one would be awake at three in the morning. When I got to the low green fence through the neighbour's property the house seemed dark, completely dead. No light or noise from inside, except a thin light from the basement shining out of a small low to the ground window, slightly ajar. This was my opportunity, I thought. If Lincoln were in there, I could sneak him out.

After breaking up the space cake and scattering it over the fence, I waited an hour, hearing their salivating jowls vacuum up every last crumb. I took sneak peaks over the fence to review progress. Within thirty minutes they were slowing down. One dog in particular stared at the fence with a low-pitched moan, then wobbled, slumping down on his haunches. By the time I counted four stoned lumps on the lawn I climbed over, crept like a ninja, got down on all fours to get a peek through the window – concrete floor and walls and one lonely Lincoln restrained, gagged, nodding off but not quite falling asleep. Then came the blow to my head.

"Three!"

He pulls away. I look down, there's no blood, no pain. I'm not sure whether to laugh or cry. My nuts are still there but the nutcracker remains snugly in place. He grins, paces the basement glaring at me, then returns to whisper in my ear. "Soon, my friend." He pats me on the head. "I promise. It's just a little early. It would spoil the ending."

He goes back to the toolbox, rummages around and pulls out a strap on rubber cock – the size and shape of a nine-inch, two-inch girth truncheon. A dark relief washes over me when he's moves in the direction of Lincoln. He adjusts the straps and pulls it over Lincoln's head so that the rubber cock stands erect just above his brow. Kane takes a step back like he's examining art, smiles. "I always thought you were a prized dickhead, mate."

Lincoln looks at me, wide eyed. All the promises he made, all his compelling confidence gone – dragged into a dark and foreboding black hole. The gravity of our situation is such that no light or hope could ever escape. I look at him, then we both turn to our sordid tormentor. I'm trying to block out thoughts of what's next on his macabre menu. Kane circles him, pats him on the head. "You're going to need a bit of lubing. Don't you think, dickhead?"

Lincoln strains his eyes upwards to get a glimpse of his new phallic member. I'm hoping I'm left out of this equation. I'd rather opt for what's next on the list, although it's a hard pick if it involves excising my testicles.

Kane produces a tube of KY and applies it lavishly to the rubber head and along the shaft. He wipes his greasy hands on Lincoln's sleeve, baring a dark morbid grin as he stares at me. "Don't worry, there's plenty more where that came from, so if it gets a bit a dry, a bit rough, you just nod, okay?"

I don't nod this time; fear has reached saturation. I'm realising for the first time that fear is inextricably linked to hope. You're only afraid when you are about to lose something, but when the last thing you lose is hope, then fear gives way to a stronger, bolder emotion. Hate. It's easier to hate than to wonder if this could have been avoided. Perhaps if my mother hadn't kicked me out of home, I wouldn't have been so willing to go along on this trip in the first place. It's easier to hate than to admit my stupidity in believing we could've actually got away with this.

Kane sits down on the chair, reaches into his pocket and pulls out a Chupa Chup lollipop – cola flavoured by the colour of the wrapper. He unwraps it slowly.

"Now, you faggots. I want a freak show." He pauses, looks at us. "Dickhead, I want you to break him in. Break him in real good, till he bleeds. And while you're down on your knees, I'm going to be busy myself, violating your arsehole. You fuck him in the arse. I fuck you in the arse. Got it?" He starts to suck on his lollipop, sucks it hard, pulls it out and darts his tongue around it aggressively, moans. "Mmmm… you fudge packers are going to have one hell of a ride." He stands and walks over to the corner, picks up a thick rusted iron rod. He turns to Lincoln. "This is what I'm going to insert into you, okay, buddy? What do you think?" He sucks more on his lollipop, removes it to speak. "You like, you want this big boy. You want it hard?" He circles him, comes up close to his ear. "Don't worry, I'll use protection." He tears open a condom and rolls it over one end of the rod, jabs it in the air with both hands practising his stroke, then laughs, arching his back with the lollipop still cradled in his mouth.

The laughter suddenly mutes.

He straightens, involuntarily. Obviously he hadn't intended for this to happen. He drops the rod. His eyes have changed. Fear has come to visit those eyes. He removes the lollipop from his mouth, but he's staring at what is now just a blank stick. The candy ball has gone – that sweet little candy ball is not there.

Hate has somewhere to park itself.

He clutches his throat. His face is screaming, but not a syllable of sound leaves his mouth. He's asphyxiating, eyes bulging and pleading for help. We couldn't be more perfectly disabled to watch his silent demise. Our limbs are tied, our emotions primed. Lincoln and I glance at each other in disbelief – is this really happening?

Kane tries to impale himself on the chair. It has zero effect. He thumps at his stomach, cranes over. His complexion turns crimson. A dust of blue spreads across his lips. With a last ditch effort, he reaches for the stairs, perhaps in hope of raising the alarm. He staggers up and we hear him fall at the top – a resigning thump then sliding slowly, hitting each step… thump… thump… thump…

His lower legs arrive at the bottom of the stairwell, twitching.

More twitching…

Then all goes eerily still.

Our ears are pricked, our senses calibrated to any movement coming from upstairs. There's nothing, apart from the throbbing adrenaline pulsing in my ears and the simplest, most primal thought – *I want to live*.

Lincoln mumbles something, tries to communicate with his eyes, nudging his head in a particular direction. But it's more the giant erection strapped to his head that's doing the pointing. It's the Stanley knife he wants. He begins to shuffle his chair, scraping along a millimetre at a time. I join in the effort. It's slow painful work but we're making progress, a few centimetres at a time – a miniaturised hopping technique, similar to that of a one-legged flea.

Lincoln stops, like he's contemplating. He mumbles something then keels over sideways on his chair hitting the concrete *smack* on his left shoulder. He squirms in pain. That's got to hurt, but it's a good landing. The Stanley knife is directly behind him, a foot from his bound hands which are searching blindly for it. He tries to move on his side, a pathetic wormlike action. You can hear him straining, muted screams under the gag. Then he goes quiet, his rib cage filling with recovery breaths, his nostrils flaring.

My mission, I guess, is to stay upright if this is going to work. I start flea hopping in my chair again and get my foot to just nudge the knife, sending it into a slow spinning skid as it hits the back of his hand. He gropes for it, picks it up with a secure grip. With his other hand he feels for the blade but the angle required of his wrists is too great to saw through the rope. I shuffle closer to his hands. I think he gets what I'm trying to do as my right foot comes into contact with his backside. He finds my ankle, feels around for the rope, then the blade slices slowly through each thread. Finally, my leg is freed. I shift my other foot around with relative ease and free up that leg so that now I'm standing bent over with the chair still strapped to my arse, halfway to completing my Houdini.

I kneel down and collapse next to Lincoln, our chairs back to back, our hands connecting. He manages to saw through the rope around my wrists, and our Lotto numbers come crashing down. I'm untying the rope around my waist, freeing myself from the chair, peeling off the gag, spitting out the sock. My mouth tingles as it returns to its normal shape. Then I untie Lincoln. He gets up slowly, straightening his legs from a forty-eight-hour ordeal. He tries to say something but his stretched mouth struggles to shape the words. I have to support him till he finds his feet, then we stumble towards the stairwell picking up our clothes. "Led's ged da fug outa here," he slurs, stepping over Kane's body. I glance down. His last expression is that of a swollen blue-tongued lizard.

"Hey, you've still got that head gear on," I remind him.

"Uh? Shidd." Lincoln pulls it off and jams the rubber cock right down Kane's throat. It makes a horrible gurgling sound. "Sug on dat, cocksucker." And we're up the stairs and out into the absolutely positively Wellington air.

71

13

No one's following. We slow to a steady stroll across the Basin Reserve in the early hours of what now must be Monday morning.

I ought to be relieved, at least grateful to have a future however small and uncertain, but there's a fresh image in my head that is taking time to process. The face of a dead man. A person *actually* died tonight.

Lincoln's speech is starting to return to normal. "Good one, man," he says, then after a pause, "Thank you."

"For what?"

"Rescuing my arse. Although I knew he was just waiting for you to turn up."

"What happened before I showed? You didn't tell them about me, did you?"

He shakes his head. "Relax. With Kane gone, you're still unknown."

I look down at the ground. This is my moment. Time to go our separate ways. Nothing good could come from hanging around someone who is now more of a marked man than ever. I stay composed, realising the perpetual seriousness of the situation. "What are you going to do?" I ask.

His eyes widen. "Don't you mean, what are 'we' going to do? You're still in, aren't you?"

"Yeah, but... I just thought I could take my cut now, kinda split."

"Like the hell you're going to take your cut." There's bitterness in his voice. "We're not clear yet."

"Yes... but... I thought you said they don't know I'm involved."

"That's right," he says. "But you do realise if they hunt me down and find me, what do you think will happen?"

I try to imagine but there's a thought block. "You tell me?"

He sighs. "Let me fill you in. They will torture the fuck out of me until I relinquish your name. Then they will come after *you*. Do you think they're going to be happy with just their money back? Fuck no. They will be out for blood. Our blood. Do you understand?"

Now I feel like screaming. "What the hell have you got me into?"

He smiles condescendingly. "Wake the hell up. Don't be so naïve. You shook on this, remember?"

I hate that he's right. Now I want to go back to the start, back to the feeling of safety behind the line, where my life wasn't so bad – maybe a little beige but a damn sight better than this nightmare. I say nothing to this, just walk.

"Where are we heading by the way?" he asks.

I sigh. "Back to the hotel."

14

I just want to retire when I get in. I'm lying on the bed pretending to sleep while Lincoln paces the room. It seems there is not one minute of respite less than before. "It's out of the frying pan and into the fire," he says. "We need to get going, before they wake and find Kane." He stops, then paces more, back and forth. "What happened to that car," he asks. "Did you buy it?"

I keep my eyes closed. "Yeah. Helen's got it."

"What?"

I open my eyes and sit up. "I can't drive, remember? What else was I going to do with it?"

He ponders a moment. "Where is she now?"

I shrug. "You can call her if you like. I have her number."

"Give," he commands. "If we hurry we could catch the early Picton ferry."

I stall, handing him the number. "You might want to know something before you call her."

"What?" he says, impatient.

"Well, I had to tell her something."

His eyes widen. "You didn't tell her about the money, did you?"

I shake my head, dreading how I'm going to explain this. "No. It's not that. I told her the reason you disappeared is because, you really liked her."

He shrugs. "Yeah, so?"

I sigh, shrink further into my shoes. "Well, I told her you have emotional issues, when it comes to relationships. A kind of mental illness."

"You fucking said what?"

"In all fairness, what else could I have said?"

"You could have told her my grandmother died or something like that."

I swallow. "Yeah, that would have been better, I guess."

"Fucking emotional issues, unbelievable."

It's six a.m. when he phones Helen. Lincoln gives the dying grandmother story routine, which she seems to accept as he paces with the cordless phone to his ear. "So, you still want to come with us?" He winks at me. "Excellent, but you need to be here," he glances at his watch, "in say forty-five minutes, can you do that?" There's a pause and another wink. "Okay, see you soon, babe," and he rings off.

Helen's parked in the drop off zone out front. She seems pleased to see us, and I'm genuinely pleased to see her despite knowing she is now getting more entangled into our mess. Lincoln slides into the back of the Skoda. I take the front passenger seat with my pack wedged between my legs. Helen seems to have questions and stalls before turning the ignition.

"We haven't got much time," Lincoln says.

Helen shrugs, puts it in gear. "All right then. South Island here we come." She turns right onto Lambton Quay.

I can sense the awkward collision of worlds. I have the urge to spill the beans to her. It would only be fair to let her know what she's really getting into, just to add a modicum of decency to the situation. But as the equation stands this is more about survival than the past moral compass I used to steer by. Nevertheless, I feel like stirring the pot a little. I look over my shoulder at Lincoln. "I'm pretty excited about this trip, aren't you, buddy?" He doesn't answer, distracted, checking behind for anyone following.

"So," she says, stopping at a red light. "How did the funeral go?"

The lights change. I'm hiding my grin, more out of a coping mechanism to deal with the chain of lies that are about to unravel.

"Oh, it went okay, I guess." Then a little pause for effect. "She was cremated."

This seems clever from Lincoln, it's not like she would then ask how the burning went. She refrains from asking more questions and just drives.

15

There's still time when we pull into the ferry terminal. Lincoln's gone to purchase the tickets while we sit in a long queue of cars waiting to board. It's just Helen and myself and a forbidden silence between us, like we're not supposed to talk to each other, that somehow this could be classed as intimacy.

I'm about to say something when she fires first. "So, you've been planning this trip long?"

"Yes and no," I reply, shaking my head. "I mean... I've been wanting to take this trip but there wasn't much planning. I kind of got kicked out of home, a couple of days ago."

"Really," she says. "Go on."

"Go on what?"

Those delightful dimples appear with her grin. "What happened, what did you do?"

I hesitate, only because I'm not sure whether I've formulated it right in my mind yet. "You know, just the usual pressure from parents. Have to get a job, be responsible and stuff."

She shakes her head. "No idea what you're talking about."

"You don't get that from your olds?"

"Not since I left home, like as soon as I could." She looks at me. "What took you so long?"

I shrug. "I guess I was too comfortable. As long as they left me alone I was all right. But once I finished my studies it was all about, what next, when was I going to look for work."

She nods. "Yeah, that's what most parents do."

"Yeah, but in my case I'm an only child, so they have always expected a lot from me, like I'm going to be this big career person or something." I stare out the window and watch a forklift driver manoeuvre a loaded pellet. "What's the rush anyway. Look out there, look at all those people working their arses off living from pay check to pay check. What's the point of it?"

"So, they kicked you out for being a slacker?"

I sigh. "Not just that. I kind of got really mad. My mother, she started nagging all the time about the smallest stuff." I hesitate. "It was her cabbages, in the end, that's what clinched it."

She frowns. "The cabbages?"

"I hung out my washing without pegs. She was always on at me for not using pegs. The wind got up and she found my underwear strewn through her cabbage patch."

Helen laughs.

"I'm serious. It really got her goat up. She came right at me, red with anger, and I just thought, this was totally unnecessary – a complete overreaction. Usually I just wore it and didn't argue, but this time all her nagging suddenly snowballed on me. I blew up. Started swearing and saying pretty nasty stuff."

"And then?"

"Well, she hadn't heard anything like it. Up till then I never really rocked the boat. It came as a major shock to her. She started crying and screaming, all hell broke loose. She began emptying my room, throwing my clothes out the window." I pause to reflect. "It was a relief actually, perfect timing, as it turned out."

Helen nods. "So that's how you got here. Pretty happenstance."

"Yeah. Lincoln was looking for someone to head south with. I just happened to be perfectly available."

She laughs. "Geez, and I thought I was the impulsive one. This whole thing is more random than I thought."

"You know, it's not too late if you want to bail," I say.

Helen looks at me with surprise. "You sick of me already?"

"Not at all. I love your company." I feel myself blush a little, perhaps I should have said *like* instead of *love*. "I mean you're pretty easy to have around."

"Thanks," she says. "Anyway, there's no way I'm bailing now. The only thing that could put me off is if you two turn out to be a couple of psychos." She laughs. I laugh along, but perhaps a little more forced. I study the clock on the dashboard. Lincoln should be back by now. Up ahead I notice a guy walking along checking the cars as he goes. I sit up. He's not in uniform, definitely not a ferry worker. As he gets closer, I want to believe that my eyes are deceiving me. But it's pretty obvious by the gang regalia and heavy swagger who he's looking for. I want to run, every cell in my body is on standby, however running would be the worst thing I could do right now. Just relax, I tell myself. Play it cool. Whatever you do don't look at him. He's a few cars away. I turn to Helen. "So, have you ever been to the South Island before?"

"Yeah, heaps of times."

I force a smile and train my eyes on her face. "What do you like about it?"

She shrugs. "What's not to like? Mountains, fresh air, spectacular beaches..." She goes on telling me about past South Island trips and I'm not listening at all, deafened by the throbbing fear pulsing in my ears.

Helen suddenly stops midsentence. Her face goes flat. Every nerve in my body is on standby. "What is it?" I ask.

"There's a guy looking through the window, directly behind you." I turn slowly. Black wraparound sunglasses and a hard pitted face is staring straight at me, but with the added feature of planet Saturn tattooed on his forehead. I'm about to revisit the realms of past trauma, on the verge of soiling my undies. I wind down the window. "Can I help you?"

The Saturn rings wrinkle as he smiles. "Nah," he says, and walks on.

"Who the hell was that?" Helen asks.

I start breathing again, shrug, "I have no idea, but the main thing is he's gone." I look around to see if I can spot Lincoln. He's nowhere.

A few minutes go by and the cars in front start to move. "Shit, where the hell is he?" Helen has no choice but to start the engine. She's about to put it in gear when the back door opens and in slides Lincoln. I look over my shoulder; he's crouched slightly, shaken, out of breath. "Sorry, there was a bit of a queue for the tickets."

Helen smiles, edges the car forward. "Talk about cutting it fine."

16

We're on the top deck when we feel the boat start to pull out from the pier. Something inside me also departs – perhaps from all things naïve and moral abandoned on the shore.

Lincoln and I decide to head to the bar while Helen has gone off to the ladies. After that she plans to call her friend and tell her where she's at.

We're the only ones drinking at nine in the morning. Lincoln turns to me, lifts his beer. "Cheers," he says, but not smiling. He looks edgy, slightly pale as if his tan has suddenly grown legs and walked off his face.

I take up a barstool and pick up my beer. "What are we drinking to?" I ask. "Is it something to do with your mate back there? The guy with a Saturn tattoo?"

He takes a heavy swig of his beer, looks down. "You mean Hohepa Jones."

"Who's he?"

He puts his bottle down, makes sure I'm listening. "Look. Things have changed."

I shrug. "What's changed? Last time I checked we were being hunted like animals."

He shakes his head. "No. This is different. If you think Kane was bad, this guy is infinitely worse. I met him once. This guy is the incarnation of the Devil, man. He's a freak."

I smile nervously. "Great, sounds fab. Another one of your psychopathic gang buddies, can't wait to meet him. I love what you've got me involved with here. Nice." I lift the bottle to my lips, take several gulps, drain half the beer before setting it down. "Fuck, Lincoln, where the hell did you find these guys, a horror movie?"

The barman glances at us. Lincoln signals to me that we should take our beers outside.

We're leaving the harbour now, bearing towards the Cook Strait. The heads of the harbour mouth are dotted with small white fishing boats, bobbing vulnerably on the edge of the great Southern Ocean. We lean over the rail; a salty breeze hits our faces. I've been yearning for this moment for some time, cut off from the frenetic pace of the North Island. My heart has always belonged in the South. Every trip I've made there has stuck in my memory.

"So, about this guy Hohepa. Did he see you?"

Lincoln hugs his beer with both hands. "I don't think so. I saw him coming, had to think quickly; hid behind a cargo truck and waited until it was clear." He sips his beer thoughtfully. "You know, this guy Hohepa, he's not going to stop, he's never going to stop until I'm buried ten feet under. Killing one of their gang is like killing a member of their family. It's their own blood you know. You do understand that?"

I shake my head. "We didn't do shit. He choked himself to death."

"He won't see it like that, and you know it. And what really bugs me is I didn't expect he'd be on to us so early. He's like a blood hound, knows exactly where to go sniffing."

"Well, maybe if you didn't shove a rubber cock down the guy's throat then accidental choking may have been considered." I look down at the waves crashing off the hull. "You sure he didn't see you?"

Lincoln looks at me square in the eyes. "Put it this way, if he had seen me, I wouldn't be talking to you right now. This guy doesn't give a fuck about going to jail. He'll eat you alive, on the spot." He pauses. "I'm not sure whether I should be telling this, but..." He hesitates.

"You're already telling me, continue."

"No, I mean, what he does to people when he finds them. And he does find them, he never fails."

When I look down, I see my hands trembling, in a bad way like the nerves themselves are going to spontaneously combust. I should have left him when I could. "Shit," I say. "You can keep the money."

Lincoln laughs. "You really don't understand, do you?"

I stand directly in front of him. "Of course I do. Hanging out with you is leading to nothing but a premature end."

"Listen, buddy." He pokes a finger into my chest. "Listen to me carefully. The money is the only thing that's going to keep you alive. This guy, if he finds me, has ways – creative fuckin' evil ways of making people talk. I'm not saying he's going to catch me, but if he does you can be rest assured you'll be next. Better we stick together on this one."

"What exactly does he do that's so bad?"

He shakes his head. "I don't think you really want to know. It'll give you nightmares."

"Listen." I grab him tightly by the shoulder. "You need to be straight up with me. No bullshit this time. I mean, what's stopping me from leaving, taking my chances? I could fly overseas, never come back."

He shakes free of my grip. "Go ahead, try it. You don't think that maybe, after they find me they won't come after your family, squeeze whatever hurts? It would be a suicide mission."

"Yeah, but you could do the same, catch a flight, skip the country. It's not like we can't afford it."

He shakes his head. "I've thought about that. Thing is, Kurt. First we've got to get all that cash past the sniffer dogs."

"Yeah, so? Worth the risk ain't it?"

He sighs. "Then there is the issue of my arrest. I've got a warrant out on me. I breached bail, failed to turn up to court. As soon as I hand over my passport they'll nab me at customs. Then I'll be in custody, on remand, and you know they have connections inside. I'd be dead meat."

"Hey, wait a minute. I can't believe I'm hearing this shit. You're a convict?"

He shrugs. "Nothing that bad. Just for supply. Class C drugs, mainly."

I look away, briefly. "Nothing that bad, huh? Fucking Christ." I shake my head. "This is just getting better. What now? What's next in your highly organised plan?"

He pauses. I'm thinking this had better be good.

"I know a place," he says, with a confident air. "It would be the last place he'll come looking."

"And if he finds us there, what is he going to do that I haven't already experienced in the last twenty-four hours?"

He grins. "You really want to know, don't you?"

I nod. "No bullshit, Lincoln."

He sighs, looks away to the horizon. "He's going to cook you up and clean the meat off your bones." He turns his eyes on me. "You understand? He's not human. What kind of guy tattoos Saturn on his forehead? I'll tell you what kind of guy. Someone who thinks he's a cosmic God, who believes by eating you he is saving your soul. This guy is nasty sick, man. He thinks he's saving you, comprehend?"

I nod, then start shaking my head. "How do you know this stuff? I mean…"

Lincoln leans closer. "After he's done with you, he eats the evidence. He's a hired killer. 'The Termite' they call him. You want to know how he cooks you, how he prepares your slabs of meat?"

"Okay," I say, running a hand nervously through my hair. "I get it. What do we do after getting to this hideout?"

"Let's just focus on getting there first. Then we'll have the luxury of thinking without being hunted, okay?"

I nod. "Yeah, all right, understand."

Lincoln lifts his beer. "Let's have a good luck toast."

"To what?" says a voice from behind. Helen steps out onto the deck, slings an arm around Lincoln. She beams, "Hey, is anyone going to buy *me* a drink?"

17

From pitching and rolling on the Cook Strait we glide into calmer waters. We gather on the foredeck to look out over the glassy reflection of the Marlborough Sound. Usually I would feel yearning for this land, but now there's nothing but cold dread churning in my stomach.

Lincoln's chatting intimately with Helen, leaning in close, whispering in her ear. I know this shouldn't bother me. What right do I have to feeling uncomfortable? I'm out of the equation. Feeling jealous is absurd. The best thing I can do is erase any sense of this. Delete, delete. But if I'm not thinking about that then I'm thinking of Kane's face on repeat, choking my air, and then the idea of Hohepa completely dries the back of my throat so that it hurts to swallow. It seems the only thing that's stopping me from falling apart is Lincoln's grin. I don't know how he does it. He's grinning like a car salesman. I'm not sure what exactly he's selling, but it's confidence nonetheless that lends a glimmer of hope.

Disembarking goes well, as in no one seems to be following. Lincoln's driving with Helen up front in the passenger seat. I'm trying to find the off switch in my brain. The one where everything goes back to normal. I stare out the window, try to appreciate the scenery. We're actually in the South Island, but everything feels too distant to enjoy. I notice Helen's rubbing Lincoln's leg. I'm starting to think this is going to be a long ride when just a few kilometres out of Picton, Lincoln makes a sudden turn in the direction of Nelson. He glances back at me and winks. I'm assuming this is a positive sign, that the plan in his head is going well, whatever it is he's got in there. I wasn't able to pin him down earlier as to where this particular place was. All Helen is aware of is that we're going to Golden Bay.

I butt into their conversation. "Don't mean to be rude, but where are we heading?"

Lincoln eyes me in the rear vision mirror and looks away. "I already told you, man. Golden Bay."

"Yeah, but where exactly?"

"Takaka. I know a campground there, Hangdog – an under the radar kind of place. Heard of it?"

"Yeah, I've heard of it."

I look out the window at a forest of pine trees spiking the skyline. I've always wanted to go to Hangdog; everyone who's been there comes back raving more about the campground itself than the actual climbing, like there is some new and exciting life to be had there.

"Sounds interesting," Helen remarks. "So, what exactly is this place?"

"A climbers' campground. Strictly for climbers," I tell her, trying a last ditch attempt at saving her from joining us.

"Rubbish," Lincoln says. "Don't listen to him. The camp is on private property. The owner, Sid, just wants to make sure that people staying on his land adhere to a kind of culture – a climbing culture. Not a scene littered with wannabe hippies."

"I've always wanted to try climbing," Helen says. "Is it hard?"

"I'll teach you," Lincoln says, caressing her leg. "We'll borrow a harness, it'll be sweet. Besides, we have a few weeks to kill before The Gathering." He smiles at her. "You'll love Hangdog, trust me. It's like no other place you've ever stayed."

I sit back, make myself comfortable. Knowing there's a destination settles my thoughts – a safe haven on the horizon. All I have to do is sit here, nothing else. The past forty-eight hours have been a train wreck. I close my eyes and drift off to the soothing hum of the car.

18

We're ascending the Takaka Hill when I come to. The road is just as steep and windy as I remember it – something like two hundred bends you have to negotiate. This is the only way into Golden Bay and the only way out, shut off completely by the surrounding mountains of Kahurangi, so that when you begin to descend a whole valley opens up – a lost world lush with green, and a shimmering river splitting it in two snaking all the way to the Tasman and golden sand beaches. This is a place where the picture postcards don't lie.

The descent comes with the smell of burning rubber. Lincoln is trying his best at driving us off the road. There is no way of steering a two tonne East European tank down this hill, at this speed, without error. The error is coming, I can feel it. Someone should tell him to slow down, but it won't be coming from me. Here it comes, the lightness on the back wheels, the terror of that floating traction. Every cell inside me comes alive, embalmed in that sweet warmth of adrenaline. The present moment expands to encompass my simple existence. There is no future, no past, no meaning. There is no need to do anything except breathe. This could go either way. Skid left and there's a drop into a valley so perilous it would rip the skin off our bones. We're moving left, here comes our doom. We're skidding right. Helen screams, "Lincoln!" A quick handbrake, the murderous squeal of tyres and he spins the car sideways, coming to halt in the middle of the road.

I would have volunteered a scream, but I've been sitting on this formidable edge for a while now and it's no more unsettling than a spilt cup of tea. Helen is shaken up, her voice weak and tremulous. "Fuck, Lincoln, you need to slow down."

"Sorry, babe," he says, grinning as he calmly puts it in gear. "I'll slow down."

19

A few kilometres along the base of the valley and Lincoln slows to make a right turn down a gravel road. We stop at a closed gate. Attached to the gate is a hand-painted sign *HANGDOG. FULLY FULL, MAN!*

I shake my head, sigh. "Just our luck." Lincoln gets out and opens the gate anyway. "But it says full."

He gets back in the car. "Don't worry about it. That sign is always there. It's to assure the council, that's all. He's only allowed thirty punters on his land, max."

Turning the bend, we're greeted by a paddock filled with small climbers' tents and blue tarpaulins strung up between the trees. It looks more like sixty or seventy people camped out here. Everyone is either in the shade of a tree or under a blue tarp sheltering from the sun. We get out of the car. There's the sound of bongo drums in the background, a gentle human sound of guitar and laughter and friendly chatter. A definite bohemian vibe going on here, a sanctuary perhaps. This will do. I can already feel the edge dissolving.

"This place looks awesome." Helen beams.

I sigh. We're here, still breathing, still with a chance, and besides, we're in Golden Bay, disconnected from the rest of the world. Dare I say we're reasonably safe for now.

We find a patch of grass in a shady alcove bordered by trees. There's only one other tent in this area and it seems relatively hidden from the main road. While pitching the tent Helen discovers a small wooden sign camouflaged in the long grass. "Look, guys, look what it says." She points at it.

SCUMBAG CORNER

How appropriate, I'm thinking. Maybe I've reached the status of scumbag. I look at the two-person tent and at the three of us. "I guess I'll be sleeping in the car then. You love birds go ahead." Helen reddens a little and I realise I probably shouldn't have said that. Things are still pretty fresh between them.

"Hey, don't we need to sign-in or something?" I ask, unpacking our things.

Lincoln shakes his head. "No signing-in. Sid doesn't even keep a record of people coming and going." He winks at me and I get it. "The camp runs on honesty. But I think we should at least introduce ourselves."

Sid's house is set back behind a six-foot hedge which surrounds his property – private enough to keep the punters out. There's no office, just his front door left wide open. Lincoln calls out. There's a brief silence, then stomping footsteps can be heard followed by a loud Pommy voice. "Who goes there?"

Helen and I look at each other, a little bemused. A male figure appears in the doorway. I had imagined him to appear eccentric, but from what he's wearing I have to purse my lips to keep from smiling. He's fitted out in a uniform of sorts – the kind you might find on a British imperialist redcoat soldier, except that he's got long grey hair sticking out like a scarecrow under his hat and sandals fitted to his feet. He looks completely insane. I'm uncertain as to whether this is a joke or if this is what he's really like. He scans us up and down. "What do you want?"

Lincoln grins. "Hey, Sid, not sure whether you remember me from last year. I'm Lincoln... and this is Kurt and Helen."

"Hi," I say.

"Hi ya," Helen says.

Sid eyes us suspiciously. "You're not turncoats, are you?"

Helen can't hold it together, has to look away to hide her grin. I'm still uncertain about this scene.

Sid smiles a little, creasing his laugh lines, stands to attention and salutes. "Elf's Imperial Army. Lieutenant is my rank." He draws a sword made of cardboard, points it at us. "You're not anti-imperialists, are you?"

We shake our heads, grinning.

"Good. You're allowed to stay here then." He lowers his sword. "There are some basic rules, though. Four dollars a night. No loud music, especially not that electronic crap. Human music's okay. Other than that, if you want to party I recommend down by the river, as far away from me as possible. Any questions?"

We shake our heads.

"Good. Oh," he says, before turning. "There's just one more thing. Any of you happen to have any hash?"

We look at each other blankly. Lincoln pipes up. "We've got weed if you want some of that?"

Sid frowns. "Ha! That stuff is for hare brains." He laughs and walks off. We hear him holler down the hall. "Remember what the dormouse said!"

Returning to Scumbag Corner I'm still getting to grips with Sid's eccentricity. It's intriguing, especially from someone my parents' age and a camp owner. My mood is already starting to lift – nothing bad could happen here – it's a chilled-out scene, a sweet vibe.

Lincoln and Helen hop inside the tent and zip up. This leaves me alone, somewhat awkward, sitting at a picnic table, but not for long. A look-a-like Jesus with long dreads ducks his head through the branches and enters the clearing, bare-chested. "Hey," he says, approaching. "I see I've got a neighbour at last." He offers his hand. "The name's Pete."

We shake hands and I introduce myself. He sits down opposite me, just sits there smiling and saying nothing.

"There are others with me," I tell him.

"Oh yeah."

I point at the tent and make the international sign for screwing.

"Oh, right," he says, stretching his smile even further. "You want a hippie speed ball?"

"Sure, if you can tell me what it is."

"A bong followed by a shot of espresso."

I nod approvingly and he gets his gear out, including a miniature stovetop espresso maker which he manually grinds fresh beans into. It's calming to watch him prepare it with such focus and delicate artistry like it's really important to get right. "You here for the climbing?" he asks.

I hesitate. "Yeah, we're here for the climbing. And you?"

He laughs. "I was. Climbed the first two days I arrived. That was three months ago. Now I just chillax. Have a couple of hippie speed balls."

He pours the espresso into tiny shot glasses and loads the bong thick with head. "You first," he says, handing me the lighter. I take a hit, hold it in deep and exhale all the stress and worry, numbing it into submission. He does the same, although I'm sure he has none of the shit I'm dealing with, he's so chilled. "Now the espresso," he says, holding up a shot. "Cin-cin ," and down the hatch.

The coffee is bitter strong and wakes me up the way an ice-cold plunge might. "Hey, this shit really works," I tell him, feeling bright eyed and stoned. "Me like hippie speed ball."

He grins. "Excellent."

We take a couple more hits of the bong until there is no need to converse. We just sit there, basking in the sun, watching drunken woodpigeons crash through the trees, and the bongo drums start up again. I close my eyes, hold onto this feeling as long as I can. This is where I want to be. Free from being hunted, gagged, threatened, free from choices with dire consequences, free from searching for a future, free from the idea you have to make it alone in this world. This headspace I'm in, is exactly where I want to be. But it's not perfect because it won't last. It would last longer if the image of Kane wasn't so fresh, or the wrath of Hohepa so real. I'd relinquish my entire share of the money for a memory wiping machine, erasing just the last forty-eight hours but leaving a faint impression of the lesson learned.

The moment passes, and from Lincoln and Helen's tent comes a giggle and some kind of animalistic growling. The tent starts to shiver and an unmistakable repressed moan begins to grow more audible until it's too embarrassing to ignore.

Pete's smiling. "Hey, how about a swim," he suggests. "You've got to check out the river."

I nod. "Let's do it."

I follow him through the campsite, across the road and down a long thin track cut into the bush. We get halfway along when Pete stops abruptly and looks down. At his feet are pieces of screwed up paper and a torn envelope. He picks up the two halves of the envelope and connects them where they've been torn. I move in closer. "What is it, man?"

He hesitates. "This has got my name on it. It's like addressed to me." I find more of the paper strewn through the bushes. The piece I pick up reads *Bachelor of Arts, Honours in Ma...*

Pete laughs. "These are my uni degrees, man. What I've been waiting for."

Obviously someone's ripped through the mail hoping for valuables, only to find pieces of useless paper. "You said degrees, plural," I remark. "How many did you get?"

Pete lines up all the pieces of paper on the grass to exhibit his five years of scholarly effort. "Two honours degrees, one in mathematics and the other in neuroscience. I didn't attend the capping," he explains. "So, I got them to mail them to me." He stands back to admire his prize – damp, ruined, chewed at the edges, as if symbolically prepared for a vocation that is just simply not there, and probably never will be in our brave new fiscal world. "Sweet," he says. "Wow. I've got degrees, man. I'm like qualified to know shit."

I must admit I'm surprised. I'd taken Pete to be a stoned fool. "Well done," I say. "Congratulations. I guess if you ask the uni they'll send you fresh copies."

Pete shakes his head. "No need. I'll just tape them together. It would be a waste of paper otherwise. Besides, we need the trees more than degrees, yeah?"

This moment has lifted my appreciation of Pete. He seems authentic. Not many people I know can fit this mould. He gathers the fragments into a bunch and stuffs them in his pocket. He's beaming, "This calls for a celebratory joint and a jump off the top tier." It's not like I need to get more stoned, but Pete pulls a pre-rolled double-skinner from behind his ear. "Follow me," he says. The track forks off and we negotiate a steep incline, scrambling and pulling at roots, bashing our way through flax till we reach an abrupt end – a sheer cliff drop over the Takaka River.

"Come, stand out here," Pete says. He's right on the edge, his feet curled over honey-combed limestone. I sigh. That edge beckons me again. I join him, balancing over sharp ridges of rock until I can see straight down – a ten or twelve metre drop into a deep blue river hole, only there's a bush sticking out halfway and a large stone ledge at the bottom – it's this you have to clear to make it to the water. "Parabolic curve," he says to me. "That's the kind of trajectory you need for the jump. But first, my man, it's dooby time."

It doesn't take long to suck that bad boy to the roach, which Pete happily swallows at the end. He stands, carefully balancing on the honeycomb ridges and gives a mock demonstration on how to jump. "Leap out as far as you can, like a bat, then before hitting the water, point the heels and fold in your arms, otherwise you'll get bitch slapped."

I nod, smile. "I'll watch you first."

Pete stops to ponder something. "You know, have you ever wondered why we do this crazy stuff? There's some pretty interesting neuroscience behind it."

"Jump already," I say.

"Just think what our grandfathers were doing at our age? They were fighting a war, right? Did you know that the best fighter pilots were men our age? These young pilots flew straight into certain death, no hesitation. At our age our pre-frontal cortex is underdeveloped. Apparently, we lack the wiring to foresee consequences." He laughs. "And knowing this I should probably compensate for my lack of judgement, right?"

Pete suddenly turns and leaps, the double honours degree stuffed in his pocket temporarily forgotten. I'm sitting too far back to view his fall, but there's an almighty splash with a bit of body slap that chills me to the bone. He's yelling, eggs me to jump. I stand in the same spot as Pete and peer down tentatively at the ledge and the bushes protruding. "Remember," he yells out. "Parabolic curve. Jump out like a bat!"

I wait until he swims clear. There's a countdown going on in my head, but it keeps resetting as I get to one. My legs are slightly bent. I'm imagining this so-called parabola. It all sounds good in theory. I stall for time. Kane's face is still on repeat, choking my thoughts, but it's the haunting vision of Hohepa standing right behind me that spurs me to jump.

There's not much bat style going on, more like flailing arms. I close in my body and welcome the dark depths below.

20

Two weeks have passed, reeling in December and a newcomer to Scumbag Corner. We've had to nickname Pete 'Hippie Pete', not to be confused with the new guy whose name is also Pete. It took a few days to work out an appropriate name for the newbie, and in the end 'Stinky Pete' or just 'Stinky' fitted well, given he arrived with no gear, no sleeping bag, no nothing, just the clothes he stood in and a bad smell. He didn't seem to have any food either, or money, but with the generosity of his neighbourly Scumbags and the outer Hangdog community, he has been fed three times a day and sleeps under a tarpaulin he found abandoned in the trees.

As for Lincoln and I, we haven't spoken much, like nothing ever happened – we just arrived in Hangdog and now it's working out – there's a sense not to disturb that. I'm afraid of jinxing the good vibe even if it is illusory. I know that the new plan is no plan, other than hunkering down. I've read it in his body language. Each time Helen suggests a trip offsite Lincoln gets all tense and distracted. Helen has at least persuaded him to take her climbing in Paynes Ford – located adjacent to Hangdog, a distance which only commits him to ten metres or so on the exposed road before ducking back into bush. Safe enough for Lincoln, I'm guessing. But with Stinky Pete lurking around, Lincoln has become nervous about the money and has hidden all of it in the inner casing of the car doors. I'm glad it's less accessible now. Before I had the tendency to sneak a peek, envisioning it as currency for a better life, but it only brought back the fear, what lies in wait for us. It's this place, this asylum from the outside world which matters now.

It's been a great distraction sampling the one hundred odd rock climbs on offer here. Each route on the limestone cliff has its own unique name and character. Elvis Lives in Takaka is one such example, and when your legs start to spasm and tremble halfway up like the King on stage, you totally get it. But for me the name has a further meaning. Given the isolation of this place, Takaka seems the ideal location to escape from your former life – a hidden sanctuary perhaps for the 'King of Rock 'n' Roll' in all of us.

As for Sid, we've rarely seen him, except for one particular day when he turned himself into a running newsreel. While the results of the US election (Gore vs Bush) came in, he darted in and out yelling updates about who was leading the race. When Gore was proposed the winner, he came out beaming. When Bush believed he was the winner, he came out laughing. To him it was all a weird joke.

On a brighter note, this morning I biked into Takaka, an easy three-kilometre journey on an old spotty bike from

Sid's fleet. He has revamped a bunch of really old bikes and painted them with pink polka dots. With just one gear, they are reminiscent of times past when you didn't need fifty gears and fancy suspension. It was a sweet ride into town, gliding past sleepy meadows dotted with buttercups and Jersey cows grazing in the sun.

I checked my exam results at an internet café when I arrived and was pleasantly surprised I had outclassed myself with passes on all my papers. So tonight, we Scumbags are celebrating, not only because I've completed my degree in Bugger All, but also to tie in Hippie Pete's scholarly achievement which he diligently dried out and glued on a piece of cardboard cut from a beer carton. It's real class. The ink has smeared, it's illegible. We've told him but he's adamant it's fine. He's even pinned it up on a tree – it resembles abstract art more than anything else.

The sun is still riding the sky. While we wait for Hippie Pete to return with a keg for tonight, we decide to take a dip in the river. We've come to learn that the best swimming time is late afternoon, when the sun has taken the ice out of the water. Lincoln and I dive in and swim to the other side. We lie with our bellies on the sun-warmed stones waiting for Helen. This has become a daily ritual and our substitute for showering most days. It gives a whole new meaning to being a scumbag.

Helen dives in and swims across to join us. I've seen her in her bikini before. Each time I'm hoping to become more desensitised to it. I try telling myself she is just one of the guys, except for the blaringly obvious fact she's smokin' hot. Every private thought, every desire I have ever had, every fantasy about the female form, can be summed up in the silhouette of her coming out of the water. She lies down next to us, and we all share a moment in silence staring out at the flow of the river.

Lincoln pipes up, "I'm going to try the Acid Test again. Anyone care to join me?"

We both shake our heads. "We'll watch and laugh," says Helen.

Lincoln stands, grins with confidence. "It's gonna go this time."

We've been witnessing his progress all week on the Acid Test – an overhanging climb over the river. Starts off horizontal and goes straight out along a six or seven metre roof of sharp and awkward holds and tense body positions. He always gets to the lip, grunts and collapses into the drink. Quite the daily entertainment. I tried a couple of days ago but was way off the strength needed. Lincoln is strong, his upper body ripped. I'm like a Mr Puniverse next to him.

Lincoln has just started out at the bottom of the roof when I ask Helen how she's liking Hangdog. She smiles. "Being here? It's the best."

"Great," I say, shaving off some guilt now that she's actually enjoying herself. "And being around climbers?" I ask, "They're not too feral?"

"Go, honey!"

She ignores me, transfixed on Lincoln as he negotiates the lip. He's huffing and puffing, looks like an upside-down monkey trying to get his feet above his head. He gets further this time, grunts, pushes down with his palms and manages to find the traction to heave himself over. We stand and whoop at his success. Lincoln's beaming and does a celebratory bomb into the water. When he returns to sit down next to us, I divert my eyes as Helen rewards him with a kiss. I'd give anything to be in his shoes right now. He seems so nonchalant about being with her, and yet she appears all-in, giving him his undivided attention.

Trying not to fall victim to the passive third wheel, I suggest the underwater rock running game. "Who's up for it?"

"Well, I'll give it a try," Helen says. "I've seen it enough times to be curious." Lincoln is already hunting out his stone so I guess we're all playing. I've been trying this game for a week now, ever since Hippie Pete showed it to me. You have to pick up the biggest rock you can carry and walk steadily into the river. If it's heavy enough you should, in theory, be able to walk the entire width of the riverbed underwater, although it's more like a run, hence the name 'underwater rock running'. The rock gets lighter the deeper you go and you have to fight against getting swept away. Hippie Pete claims he's done it. The key is apparently picking the right size rock for your body weight.

Lincoln finds a monster he can barely pick up. I've gone more conservative this time as I previously nearly dropped the damn thing on my toe. Helen gets hers and by the look of it she'll be lucky to get halfway before she gets swept into the current. We all line up along the bank. "Okay, Scumbags! On your marks. Get set. Go!"

And off we crack at a snail's pace carrying these enormous rocks. We've all got the wide-gaited waddle going on. Helen's laughing, which is a sure sign her rock isn't heavy enough. Lincoln and I couldn't laugh if we tried, our faces straining under the weight. We hit the water. Lincoln is ahead, with Helen and I close behind. Knee-deep, then waist and shoulders. The rock is getting lighter. When the water reaches the neckline, I take a deep breath and dive like a U-boat – this ensures a sudden forward thrust with the rock directly out in front of me to counteract the steep gradient and increasing weightlessness.

I can make out a blurry visual of Lincoln well ahead of me now; he's running into the centre of the river, keeping a reasonably straight line. That's the trick, you don't want to stray off or the current will take you. I'm running as well but already I'm feeling weightlessness creeping in. I'm near the bottom, all I have to do is get across the lowest point and I should be able to make it. The current strengthens. I hear a loud amplified clunk behind me – the sound of Helen's stone dropping. She must be done. I maintain focus as oxygen races away from my brain. I'm moon jumping which isn't a good sign. Lincoln is already making his way up the other side – he might actually make it. I reach for my next step but I'm already floating up and the current takes me. Dropping my stone, I break the surface.

After taking a breath, I get my bearings and spot Lincoln walking up the other bank triumphantly lugging his rock. I put it in a couple of strokes to get out of the main current, only then to realise I can't see Helen. She must have swum back to the bank by now, surely? I tread water and do a 360-degree turn. I spot her, further down river, clinging onto an undercut of rock where the flow is concentrated and channelled. What the hell is she doing there? Somehow, she has got herself stuck in the only real hazard on this river. Her body is being pulled under. She's just got her head above water. I can hear her screaming, somewhat muffled by the sound of the rapids. If she lets go, she'll be toast. I should think about this but don't. I'm in the current letting the river take me straight to her. Just before I sweep under the rock, I grab on, hoping to find purchase. I get a hand on and momentarily submerge so I'm blindly groping for another hold. I'm on with both hands.

She looks across at me with a face washed in fear. I look up at the rock. It's clear to me what needs to be done. Before my arms lose strength, I heel hook with my right foot over the lip and lever down hard. This gives me access to higher holds and I'm able climb up and out of the water. Standing on a ledge, I step across to where Helen is and reach down, grabbing her under the arm. Relief comes to her face and she is able to get enough strength to hook her foot the same way and lever over. She's limp, out of breath. I let her recover a little before guiding her the rest of the way up the gentle incline.

"Not far, just a couple of metres and it should get easier." She nods, some colour returns to her pallor. I'm right behind her, pointing out foot holds. We both pull over the top and look down at what could have been. She puts her hand on my shoulder. I turn and she leans into me, trembling, a few gasps of tears. I have no idea what to do. This seems the most terrifying part of all even though officially the rescue is over. I pat her on the back, like one would a bloke, try not to rub her gently in case she thinks I'm taking advantage. Damn it – I'm now rubbing her gently. My heart's racing. She pulls away from the hug a little but still has her hands at my side. Our faces are intimately close. Her eyes are somewhat softer towards me than before. I'm paralysed by some invisible thing between us. Goose bumps populate all over my body, waiting for everything or anything to happen.

Suddenly we hear Lincoln crashing through the trees, calling out. I break away from her. She blushes, diverts her eyes. "We're over here!"

21

Back at Hangdog we've rolled in a keg of Macs and invited everyone to join us in our corner. So far it's just us Scumbags circling the keg. The sun is riding low on the horizon and I've already lost track of how much I've drunk, trying to suppress any thought of what happened earlier. Helen has been subdued about it, which is understandable given she probably saw her life flash before her eyes. I had to do most of the talking when it came to explaining what occurred. I played down my role in the rescue. I made out that she got out of danger by herself, that I was just there in case. I figured if she wanted to correct me in front of Lincoln she would, but she remained silent on the matter, avoiding eye contact as I spoke. I'm starting to think that what happened between us was just a passing moment, an intense couple of minutes with our emotions running high. Something might have happened if Lincoln hadn't come when he did. Something irreversible or harder to back out of, let alone having to explain what we were doing if Lincoln saw us. But this, I suspect, is just my thoughts running wild. I don't even know if I really wanted something to happen. It would complicate everything, let alone making illegitimate moves on someone who is clearly not available. I don't even think Helen would have wanted anything to happen judging by how distant she seems with me tonight. Best thing, I tell myself. Drink and forget about it.

It doesn't take long for the drunken energy in the group to gather momentum. The antics start with drinking games. We begin with Wiz, Boing, Bounce then into balancing tricks ranging from handstands, handsprings and standing on our head. I'm unsure how we arrive with a bucket of water trying to pick bobbing apples with our teeth. Then Lincoln suggests something we've never heard before. "Let's play Shallow Water Blackout!"

"What's that?" I ask.

He grins. "It's pretty simple. All you do is put your head in the bucket of water, completely submerge it. While holding your breath keep tapping the bucket with your hand. When your tapping slows we know you are about to pass out. That's when we pull you from the bucket."

"Sounds like drowning fun," I remark, then kick myself for saying it. I look across at Helen who's not smiling, certainly not wearing any joy on her face.

Lincoln sighs. "Look, you won't drown. That's what the tapping's for, and besides, with everyone watching nothing can go wrong."

"Yeah, well. I'm going to pass on this one," Helen says, which is no surprise. Both Petes nod, which only leaves me.

Out of respect for Helen I stall a little before answering, despite being excited as all hell to try it. I nod. "Yeah, guess I'm in."

Lincoln slaps his hands together, grins. "That decides it then."

First up on Shallow Water Blackout is Stinky. He takes a deep breath and plops his head in, keeping it submerged as he taps steadily. It's a weird sight: four of us standing around a guy with his head in a bucket, so much so that it attracts passers-by. "What's he doing?"

No one answers; all eyes are glued to the bucket. Hippie Pete is keeping time on a stopwatch. I can see this turning into a warped, if not morbid competition. It's been a minute and his tapping slows. "We should get him out," Helen suggests.

Lincoln puts his hand up defensively. "Not yet."

The tapping gets slower, then slower. Looking around at the group it doesn't seem like anyone else is worried. Why am I freaking out so much? What's wrong with me? Usually I'm a magnet to danger, and this is relatively tame in comparison to what I've been through. A face starved of oxygen is all I can envisage. After Kane I don't think I could handle looking at another. "Come on," I say, nervously.

"All right, all right," he sighs, and pulls him out by the shoulders. He gasps for breath, his face dripping. Stinky gets to her feet, smiles. "Man, why didn't you leave me there longer? I still had reserve."

Lincoln laughs. "Who's next?"

We're all looking at each other. When no one steps forward, Lincoln goes instead. "Now, don't pull me out until the tapping is really slow, okay." We all nod as he plops his head in. The stopwatch is reset.

More passers-by come to see what's going on. "It's been a minute and a half," Hippie Pete announces. The tapping is really slow by my standards. I go to pull him out and Stinky stops me. "A few more seconds," he says. He finally pulls him from the bucket as the last tap seemed faint, almost pathetic.

Lincoln's pale, he's gasping and he has to lie down for a while catching his breath. He sits up eventually. "What did I get?"

Hippie Pete consults his watch. "One minute, fifty-one seconds."

"Far out, man. I was starting to see colours."

"Ah, the tunnel of light perhaps," Stinky jokes.

Some guy who has been standing next to us, watching, decides it's his turn. In he goes with a definitive plopping sound, spilling some of the water. "Hey, that's cheating," Stinky says. "He should be disqualified for that."

The clock ticks, the tapping slows and now there's a Hangdog crowd circling with morbid fascination. I take a step back to observe this crazy scene. At our age our parents were already building careers, getting married, buying up property. Our generation has drawn down massive student loans. The best we can manage is to distract ourselves before the serious part of paying it all back, watching the minds of our generation nearly drown in a bucket of debt.

One minute thirty-four seconds he's pulled out. On a whim I decide it's my turn.

In I go, sensing the cold sealing over my face. I start tapping. This isn't so bad, kind of peaceful in here. Perhaps I could wear this bucket forever, mute the noise of the world. How long has it been, half a minute maybe? It would help if I could look at a stopwatch, give me something to focus on but instead I think of Helen again. Is she watching me do this? What's she thinking – that I'm just like the rest of these nut jobs? My chest is tightening, I'm heading into the next phase. This must be what the final throes of drowning feels like, knowing this is your last moment. Some air bubbles leak from of my mouth. *Just keep it together. Keep the tapping going. That's all I need to do.* I'm tapping, tap, tap… tapping away the rest of my life, staring at the inside of this bucket. *Hey, what if my actual brain had eyes – a separate pair of peepers I wasn't aware of. That would be kind of strange.* Tap, tap, tap… *The brain would be floating in my head, peering out at the inside of my skull, or could these eyes turn in towards the brain, start to look at my thoughts? Hell, these eyes could give me a second opinion. My own personal critic on the mind, man. The miiind, maaan*, tap…bubble, bubble… bubble….

The air and the night are force-feeding my lungs. A mess of wet hair covers my face but I'm too weak to clear it away. It takes me some time to get to my feet, to gather

115

focus in my oxygen starved brain, to work out the original point of this exercise which now seems no more than a combination of ego and an underdeveloped frontal lobe. Hippie Pete calls the time, "Two minutes, thirty-seven." Turns out, I'm vying for first place.

For the next half hour or so, the bucket witnesses a spate of attempts from the crowd, and maybe some dwindling interest given no new records are set. Finally, but not least, Hippie Pete is the last up to the crease, relinquishing his time keeping duty. No one takes over the stopwatch. The crowd seems more drawn to the keg which Stinky starts siphoning out to everyone. Hippie Pete is left unwatched with his head submerged in the bucket. I assume Lincoln is covering it, and it's by pure chance that I turn to take a leak in the bushes and see him, bent over, arms flopped to the ground, unmoving.

"*Fuck!*"

I race over and tackle him by the shoulders. The bucket spills and his whole body flops to the ground like a limp fish. "Guys, help!" They all come rushing. I flip him on his back and someone yells that I should put him in the recovery position, so we roll him to the side. His face is pasty white. Fuck, fuck! Is he breathing? Then there's a cough and Hippie Pete spews out a volume of water, spluttering to life. His eyes roll back, he's not all there. His breathing becomes more regular and we hold him as he stares blankly at the ground. No one moves. A terrible silence. He coughs a little more and we help him sit up. He's looking around like we're strangers.

"You all right, man?" Lincoln asks.

There's a pause. "Yeah, I think so." We help him to his feet but suggest he sits down for a while on the bench.

"You think we should take him to the hospital?" Helen asks.

"Nah," says Stinky. "He's fine. He's breathing. I know what he needs." He goes and pours him a beer. For what it's worth, this cheers him up a little. Hippie Pete smiles, colour returns to his face. "Far out, man. That was close." Then after a pause, "What time did I get?"

Lincoln slaps him on the back and glances at all of us. "You're definitely the winner, man. It would have been minutes. Total commitment."

I'm about to speak, then think better of it. Telling him the truth, that it was only by chance he didn't drown, probably won't benefit him anyway. Let him keep trusting humanity – it suits him.

22

The party gradually migrates to the fire circle at the back of Hangdog. The keg is completely drained but there are still bottles of wine being handed around and joints and various contraptions combusting weed. We're tightly packed, each of us renting a segment of fire that flickers orange in our faces, and behind us hangs a black velvet sky seasoned with stars.

There's a sound of friendly chatter. Sparks of garrulous laughter make everyone talk louder. I've found a conversation myself, with some space cadet who, at the outset, seems interested that I've studied philosophy. He makes the fatal mistake of asking about existentialism.

"Existentialism is about theories on existence, a group of thinkers – Nietzsche, Sartre, Heidegger – they removed God from the equation and rejected rationalism as a way of explaining human existence." I stop there; he's just looking at me blankly stroking his wispy beard. "But I guess you don't want to hear about that."

"No, it sounds… interesting dude. Go on."

I'm aware that everything I say from here on will swell with arrogance and a certain 'cock factor' that becomes increasingly present in my drunken personality. This is where I should probably stop drinking, but can't.

"Rationalism is a whore. That's what Nietzsche said, because all the philosophers before him based their argument of human existence on rational thought: Why do we exist? What's the reason for this? They rode that pony. Got it?"

He nods.

"Then Heidegger conjectured that it wasn't important to focus on the why, but whether we live an authentic existence or not. He rejected God, religion or any other organisation that prescribed a model of living. He basically said if you want to live an authentic life then do what you think is best for you, don't listen to anybody else."

He smiles. "Yeah, man. That's what I think too."

"Pity he turned out to be a German Nazi."

"Huh?"

I shrug. "Forget about what I just said. What matters is that he was kinda right. But here comes the body slam. This of course leads to this great idea of individualism. We are alone, making our own unique passage through life, and for this reason Sartre pointed out that we are, in the end, the sum of our choices. That by existing we have to make our own choices all the time. Making a choice is not just something going on inside your head. Choice is action according to Sartre. And it's not necessarily a comforting thing. Anxiety and worry about whether you're making the right choice is constant – this, Sartre says, is freedom. It's not this fluffy concept of American Hollywood freedom.

It's brutal. We are born into this world condemned to make our choices alone; we are therefore condemned to be free."

The guy is frowning, maybe I've lost him.

"Far out, dude. That's some heavy shit." He packs a bong and hands it to me. I'm about to go on about the absurd and Camus when one hit of the bong and my cognition dissolves into mellow mush. I look around, the party is still going strong with an increasing vibe in the atmosphere, only to be interrupted by Sid flying past – a blur of wild grey hair.

"Fire in the hole!" A detonator is plunged into the flames. There's a deafening crack, sparks fly. Then he throws in a handful of detonators, sending the fire into a scatter bomb. Projectiles of glowing embers disperse. People start screaming, shaking embers from their clothes, hot coals searing through puffer jackets. I clear the area. There's just a black charred spot and a clutter of empty bottles where there was a fire a second ago. Sid smiles. He's trying to communicate with us that the party is over. Observe the rules. A reminder – if you want to party, go to the river.

There's only a handful of us now, mainly Scumbags hanging onto the dream of something better to come, dragging the party and whatever alcohol we can scrounge down to the river.

The bonfire is a monster once we get it going and all of us have to stand back witnessing this inferno lighting up the whole riverbank and its endless deposits of stones piled around us. The stones feel comfortable to sit on, and I'm comfortably stoned and boozed, mesmerised by the flames licking at the night.

We've got a stereo wired to a car battery playing Sound Garden, Metallica, Rage Against the Machine. We're turning into carnal animals, bare-chested, jumping and leaping over the flames. There's a real primal atmosphere. Helen is getting into the swing of things too although she doesn't go as far as taking her top off.

As the flames die down Lincoln seizes the opportunity to douse his lower half in the river and walk across the glowing embers in his shoes. We watch as they stick and melt as he steps. The Petes and I are fool enough to join in, which inevitably leads to the precarious idea of barefoot fire walking. From my fire walking knowledge derived entirely off the TV, the coals look ash grey with perhaps a speck of orange. There are definitely no glowing embers with small blue flames when you see professionals walk effortlessly across in bare feet. Our fire is still burning hot. No one volunteers, even though it was Lincoln who proposed the idea. We all look at each other to see who dares. Maybe we've reached the end of the antics. It's just injury from here. I'm not entirely sure what's going through my mind. However, I've got a plan and I think it just might work. In theory it makes sense, just like when you wet your finger and pass it through a naked flame. Surely this could work on a grander scale?

"Where are you going?" asks Lincoln.

I don't answer as I dip myself in the river and return dripping. There's silence as all eyes wait to see what I'm about to do. My whole body is tingling with anticipation. This is beyond fear. A step into the unknown. Pure exhilaration. What money cannot buy, what society warns you of, and the exact opposite of being bored to death by the mundane torturous drip of normality. This is the point of acting on something so incredibly dodgy, the rush is intoxicatingly divine.

"Watch this, everyone!"

I jump backwards onto the embers and get quickly up on my feet. I'm satisfied for a split second, temporarily proud of my achievement. Then there's a sudden sting all over.

"Kurt!" Helen cries. "You're burning!"

It would have worked if the embers hadn't stuck to my wet skin. It acted as double-sided Sellotape, picking up every goddamn ember it came in contact with.

My immediate future is in that river.

Bounding, leaping over the stones I reach the edge and dive in. Reminiscent of an old *Roadrunner* cartoon with steam coming off the water – an audible hiss extinguishing the small fire on my back. While I'm clutching the shallow riverbed, some first aid advice comes to mind – ten minutes in cold running water, for a burn, I think. I'm lying on my front, my back submerged. "Hippie Pete," I cry out. "Time me for ten minutes!"

All of them are standing along the edge, shining in their torches. "Man, your back looks fried," Hippie Pete says. "There's like skin peeling off and shit."

Now I'm terrified, but the ice-cold water numbs the pain and I try telling myself that it's just normal to have a bit of skin peeling.

Lincoln sounds excited. "Jesus! There goes a piece of skin now. See it guys? There it goes!"

I wait the full ten minutes and get out. It feels fine, no pain. I'm bombarded with comments. "You're crazy, dude!" and "Far out, what a nutter?" and my own question circling in my head: *Why did you do that, you fool!* People are smiling and shaking their heads, collecting empty bottles and other debris of a party that is now clearly over.

We begin our walk back, climbing the bank and onto the road. The heat is returning, starts to sting like a graze. I'm putting it down to the shirt rubbing against the 'superficial' burn I must have inflicted. By the time we reach the driveway the sting is clearly cranking up the heat, as if someone's holding a hairdryer right up close to my skin. I try to sit down when I get to Scumbag Corner, but can't – something really bad is happening – it's the heat I thought couldn't get any worse and now it's as if the fire has returned. Invisible hot pokers stab into me. I'm agitated, pacing, cursing. I start screaming. "Aaaaah ... Fuck, Fuck!"

Tent zips start to open around the camp. "Settle down, dude. You're waking the neighbours," Lincoln says.

This is my response: '*Fuuuuuuuck*! I need an ambulance! I'm in fucking pain!"

Hippie Pete tries to console me by putting his hand directly on my back.

"*Fuuuuck!*" is all he gets and all I'm capable of communicating right now. They're all looking at me, a little stunned as to why I'm behaving like a lunatic.

"Shhhh," a neighbouring camper says, shining his head torch at me. "Quieten down, man. There are people sleeping." But when I give him my psycho look he backs away. No one here seems capable of helping. All I know is I can't tolerate a second more of this. I grab the car keys.

Helen blocks my path. "Where are you going?"

"To the hospital!"

"You can't drive. The closest hospital is in Nelson. There's nothing around here."

"Fuck, then I'll go to Nelson." I sidestep her but Lincoln snatches the keys off me. He's not going to let me take the loot, I'm guessing.

"Look," Helen pleads, "you're drunk, all of us are, you can't drive and we can't drive you either."

I try to grab the keys off Lincoln but he plays catch me if you can, jingling the keys away each time I try to get near him. "Give me the fucking keys!" I scream at him.

"You heard Helen, we can't do that. Just harden up!"

I feel like smashing him right now, but don't. I actually stop for a second to think. "Then give me everything you've got to kill this goddamn pain."

Hippie Pete pipes up, "I've got some Panadol."

"And there's the rest of the gin," Stinky adds, handing me the bottle.

I nod and everyone relaxes a little. A sheet of Panadol comes my way, which Hippie Pete tries to dole out one pill at a time. "Give it here." I snatch it off him and pop out four at once.

"You should only take two," Helen explains, but I'm not listening. They have no idea I'm being tortured by an invisible army stabbing swords dripped in sulphuric acid. I swallow the pills and chase it down with a swig of gin. I try to sit in the car, hoping to recline but the seat only has two positions – bolt upright or horizontal. I recoil, curse and get out of the car.

"You can have our tent," Helen offers. Lincoln is about to object when she stops him. "Look, it's only for one night, can't you see he's suffering?"

"Okay, all right," he agrees, begrudgingly.

Everyone disperses and says goodnight. I'm left alone with my burn and my bottle of gin. I lie down in the tent, on my front, try to close my eyes, but the pain is taking on a different reality. It isn't localised any more; before I could separate it from the rest of my body and focus on 'no pain thoughts'. This is something different. A thousand burning knives slicing me open. I keep expecting to turn and see flames spreading over my arms and back. Cerebral corners of my mind are screaming. Even my thoughts morph into pain. I try to distract myself with an image – a flower, my mother, blue skies – but the images combust spontaneously into a fireball. I'd rather be anywhere but here. There are a billion mayday calls coming from every cell in my body and there's nothing left to do but drink to pass out. The bottle is still half full. I lift it to my lips and claw it down my throat.

23

I'm the first Scumbag to rise, stretching my limbs to the sun. I figure everyone else should be awake to soak in this glorious day. I want to shake their tents, tell them they have nothing to worry about, especially when their skin is not burning to a bacon crisp or their mind hasn't been kidnapped by a gremlin torching every inch of their cerebral cortex.

I'm revelling in this pain free morning, rolling a dooby, treating my hangover as a long-lost friend – so light in comparison to last night's ordeal. Now all that remains is a dull throb of heat on my back.

Hippie Pete staggers out of his tent, squinting. He yawns and makes his way over to the picnic table to sit down. He doesn't say anything for a while, slowly registering the new day. I pass the joint. "Thanks," he says. He tokes and exhales. "So, how's the burn?"

I nod. "A lot better, thanks."

He glances at the large wet patch seeping through my shirt. "Can I take a look?"

"Sure, knock yourself out." I sit with my back turned to him. He has to slowly peel the shirt from the skin. "Does that hurt?"

I shake my head. "Nah."

There's a long pause.

"Fuck dude, this needs medical attention."

"How bad is it?"

"Like... really bad. You need to see a doctor or something. It might get infected."

I'm not that concerned initially, but with each Scumbag rising and taking a look, there's the same reaction – a deep furrow in their forehead followed by the comment, "Shit, that must really hurt. You need to see a doctor." Ironic that there's more concern now that the pain has gone. "Yeah, I'll mosey into Takaka soon," I tell them.

About midday I ride a spotty bike into town. Takaka is a pretty small place – two cafés, a superette, petrol station and a couple of hippie shops selling crystals. I head to the chemist. Perhaps I could get some burn cream and dress it myself.

"Do you have any burn cream?" I ask the pharmacist. He's this tall bald guy, pale with thick rimmed glasses. He glances at the map of Africa soaked on my back as I check the shelf. He adjusts his glasses on the bridge of his nose. "Well, that depends. Is the burn bigger than a fifty-cent coin?"

I pick up a tube of what appears to be what I'm looking for. "Will this do the trick?"

He studies the tube. "For sunburn, yes." He pauses, produces that same furrow on his brow. "How big is this burn you've got?"

I pull my shirt up to show him. There's a sudden urgency in his voice. "Right, you need medical attention, right away."

I roll the shirt down. "It's not that bad. I don't even feel much pain any more."

He takes his glasses off. "That's a second or third degree burn you've got there, covering a large part of your body. It's a medical emergency." He leads me out of the shop, yelling over his shoulder to his assistant. "I'm driving this guy to the medical centre!

It's about a kilometre out of town, and when I get there I don't have to wait. I'm seen immediately by two nurses and a doctor. I'm lying on my stomach, shirt off, being examined and prodded. "Can you feel that?" the doctor asks.

"Nup, nothing."

"And here?"

"Ah… that stings!"

"Good," he says. "You haven't burnt all the nerves yet."

There's a bit of discussion between them. It sounds as if the doc is unsure what treatment I need. He leaves the room and returns holding a tub of ointment. "I'm going to apply silver nitrate to your back," he tells me. "It shouldn't hurt. In fact, you should feel relief as it slows down the burning."

"What do you mean? I thought the burning would be over by now."

He starts applying thick cool globs over my back. "The burn won't stop until all your nerves are fried, then it will start into your flesh. I've got to stop the burning, you understand?"

The word flesh gets me panicking and I think of burn victims, grossly disfigured. "Will I get a scar?"

There's a pause. "Yes, probably. But the main thing is saving your nerves while you still have them." Another pause. "How did you do this, fall into a fire or something?"

"Yep."

"Well, you don't have to tell me right now. Just that you might need to disclose it on your ACC form. I'm assuming this was an accident?"

I swallow hard. "Yep."

After applying the dressing, he leaves me with the nurses to bandage my torso and roll over a fish net vest. I look like some half-mummified Freddie Mercury returned from the dead. With all the help I'm getting, the thought hits me. These nurses, the doctor, the clerk, this whole practice teems with purpose. They all have important things to do, serving out their lives as cogs in a system that before I could only condemn as mundane. Now I can only offer them respect, and in fact for the first time I'm a little envious in my cog-less condition. They leave me alone to fill out my ACC form, and where it asks to give a brief description of the how the accident happened, I write: *I was walking along and accidently fell into a fire.* Pathetic as it sounds, it's all I can procure without seeming certifiable for the looney bin – that's if I actually told them the truth. I re-read what I've written. Remarkably there may be some truth in it after all. This whole trip has been falling into a fire. Although it was no accident.

The doctor returns and examines the ACC form. He lets out a wee chuckle. "Never seen that one before." I'm conscious that I'm exuding methanol fumes so I'm pretty sure he knows this was the result of booze. "Oh well," he says. "The things we do when we're young, eh." He pauses. "How did you slow the burning?"

"I jumped into the river. It was right there."

He nods. "Lucky. If the river wasn't there it would have been a lot worse. You would have been admitted with third degree burns."

"Sounds painful."

He shakes his head. "What you went through is a lot more painful. Basically, when you get second degree it singes your nerve endings. Third degree kills the nerves completely until you don't feel a thing. If you had called us last night, we would have given you morphine. A second degree burn to a large area of the body – most painful experience you can get. How did you cope with the pain?"

I shrug. "Took a couple of Panadol."

He looks surprised. "You must have a high pain threshold."

"I have now."

Before I leave, he instructs me to take it easy. No physical exercise. No swimming. He tells me what signs to look out for with infection and books me in for re-dressing in a couple of days.

24

The burn really slows me down over the coming week. I sit around camp all wooden and perplexed as to how to fill my day. With the skin on my back being pulled into a tight scab, I can barely move, and wearing the bandage and fishnet I really look like a prized dick.

Burn Boy is the nickname I've acquired. I'm now famous around camp, trying to see the humour in it. The pain remains fresh in my memory, although the healing process has its benefits. It makes you sit and observe a lot more. Why are we all here? What's brought us to this place? There's a psychological thread connecting all of us to Hangdog, as if we're all misplaced parts separated from the greater whole. We're all a bunch of sifters, waiting at a bus stop, temporarily escaping our former lives which will reactivate as soon as we crawl back over Takaka Hill. Hippie Pete has been here for months, a mere reprieve before returning to the reality of no career and a mountain of student debt. Helen is escaping from a mundane summer job trapped in the city. Then there is Stinky – the mystery man – he arrived with nothing, appeared from nowhere as if he was on the run from something. He's not forthcoming with what exactly that is, but then again, neither are we.

The downside of being a burn victim (correction, the downside of *knowing* you inflicted burns upon yourself – to be a victim of your own stupidity) gets worse in the scorching summer when all you want to do is dive into the ice-cold river, but can't. Instead, I'm resolved to looking at it flowing past in all its tempting glory, all the while battling an itch on my back I can't quite reach. So, this morning, when Hippie Pete suggested venturing off site for a day trip, I knew this would relieve at least one day of moping and itching around camp.

By late morning we're on the road. Hippie Pete is up front driving his hippie van. Stinky is in the passenger seat while Helen and I are seated in the back on unanchored foldout beach chairs. The vibrations feel great through the aluminium frame, a precarious position should there be sudden cornering or braking. Helen seems to be in good spirits despite her recent flare up with Lincoln prior to getting into the van. Of course, he didn't share the same enthusiasm about going on the trip, at which point Helen wanted to know why, since arriving at Hangdog, he hadn't bothered to venture much further than the swimming hole. Lincoln coughed up lame excuses, avoiding getting anywhere near the truth, like it had herpes. Although herpes would be the preferred option to a run-in with Hohepa Jones. Finally, she threatened she'd go without him. Lincoln didn't put up a fight, even encouraged her to go. She mistook it for rejection and went on to question his intentions with The Gathering, but Lincoln promised he would go. I watched the truth in his throat being swallowed.

Hippie Pete pulls to the side of the road on the outskirts of Takaka, just outside an old rundown church. Being Sunday, the local congregation has assembled and you can hear them singing joyously on this clear blue day. This little white church, with a backdrop of a buttercup filled meadow and a white picket fence around it, reminds me of a movie set, somewhat staged and out of place to the bohemian vibe of Golden Bay. However, it is certain that this church was here well before any hippie grew their hair.

"Why have we stopped?" Stinky asks. "I thought we were heading straight out to the coast?"

"Were we?" asks Hippie Pete. "There is no certainty of anything in this universe."

"Jesus, what have you been smoking?" I ask.

"Weed," he says. "Although we could do with a bit of Jesus in our hearts." He smiles his big hippie grin. "How about it then?"

"Going to actual church?" Helen clarifies.

"Yeah, just for a little while. It will be great."

After a stunned silence, I say, "I think we should vote on it."

Hippie Pete shakes his head. "That'll be boring, how about let the universe decide." He pulls from his pocket a pair of dice. "One roll. If it comes up with an even number we'll continue on. If its odds we're going in."

"Sounds fair," Helen says.

I nod. "I agree, roll them." Stinky shrugs his shoulders so I'm guessing we're all in. Hippie Pete throws the dice on the dash and they roll off into the deep cosmic corners of his van. Part of me is hoping for the unknown, the less trodden path. "Odds," Hippie Pete calls.

Sunday morning church service it is. But first we smokebox the van, blaze a doob until we're all sufficiently high to face the Lord. We get out and make a slow approach toward the front of the Church. The singing gets louder.

It's packed, except for a row in the back – a vacant bench seemingly waiting just for us. We take up our position but keep standing with the congregation as they continue to sing. They're singing a familiar Christmas Carol and we surprise ourselves by how easily the words come out of our mouths. Like all these words have been drummed into us in our childhood, a subliminal immersion of Christianity in our schools, in our communities, on television and radio and all the statutory holidays governed by the birth and death of Jesus Christ. Despite this we are definitely an alien invasion on this cosy community. There's a glass wall between our worlds, and I sense it as people start to look over their shoulder noticing our presence. This is starting to feel like a very bad idea.

The next song begins. More evangelical and people start clapping and dancing. I'm plunging into the depths of a stoner's paranoia and have to look across at Hippie Pete for some kind of confirmation or reassurance. He's smiling, of course, unaffected by the atmosphere, completely unhinged and comfortable as he breaks into dance. We're getting more looks as he begins to clap and stamp his feet, singing louder with full unimpeded madness. They're probably wondering what type of freaks we are – homeless drifters from the heathen world, or lost and desperate souls needing to be saved? My arms and legs feel limp and cold with anxiety. I check the others' reaction – Helen and Stinky smile and begin to join Hippie Pete's enthusiasm – the only door to pass through if we're really going to see this out. I force myself to sing louder and get my groove on. And then it comes – the complete absurdity of what we're doing and an unshakable smile growing from within. Like something I've been holding on to has just let go and is racing away on an unravelling ball of string. Hooked either by the hysteria in the room or the pot in my veins, I try not to analyse it too much. It's just how it is right now. This is all I'm doing – being a fool in the random universe, seizing the moment where everything is just light and supercilious and doesn't demand to be known. It just is, man. A clap. We're a happy clap in the history of time. Amen.

But the moment doesn't last. The rambling thoughts creep back when we are seated and the pastor of the church, a fit looking bearded man, closes the service with a prayer. I wonder who he's praying to. No, actually, I'm trying to visualise the man in the clouds. God with his big hippie beard and bare feet and fisherman pants, rambling to himself over the infinite conundrum of freewill, of having to listen to all those prayers but not able to answer or intervene to any of them. It must be torture. His own kind of hell. Then it hits me. No one ever sends a prayer for him – for his own salvation from the horror of listening in to all the desperation of mankind. *Dear God, it's not your fault you can't do jack. Complain higher up, take it to upper management. There must be a higher entity in charge of this circus. Amen.*

The service finishes and we are left to mingle with the congregation. The pastor makes a beeline straight for us with a big friendly smile, big teeth and handshake. "Hi, I'm Jim," he says. "You must be out of towners. Where are you from?"

We all reciprocate handshakes and introduce ourselves. "We're from all parts of the country, I guess," Hippie Pete explains, "but currently from Hangdog."

"Aha!" he says. "So, you're rockies?"

Hippie Pete shrugs. "Huh?"

"Rock climbers," he elaborates. "It's what we call you guys down the road."

We all smile, nod.

"I used to be a rocky once. When I was younger. Loved it. Just a bit hard on the old body now. What do you think of the climbing here?"

"Oh, it's great, the best." Hippie Pete smiles.

"Well, be sure to come and visit us again. And please, feel free to stick around for a cuppa." He smiles with his perfect, straight, dogmatic teeth.

"Thanks, we appreciate it."

We each take our turn to get our complimentary cup of tea and Superwine biscuit from the servery, except when it's Stinky's turn he takes a handful of Superwines to satisfy his munchies only to realise what he's doing at the last minute and puts one back. My eyes keep travelling around the room at the many religious paraphernalia hanging on the walls. The gloomy Jesus Christ nailed to the cross, looking up at God knows what. It's twisted enough that a father would send his only son to be crucified. This religion seems to be filled with pain and suffering and the great meaning of it all. Where is all the comedy, the good old laugh at our absurd existence? How does their God explain the meaning of letting rip a great big untimely fart at the dinner table, or the nincompoop leader of the world stuttering his words, or the insanity of two armies praying to wipe the other out in the name of God, or the miniscule, almost non-existent blue dot we call Earth in the billions and trillions of planets and suns in the infinite belly of time? No answer, none at all, just the nonsensical vague blabbering of the Bible, corruption at the highest level, and I don't even want to begin about what happened to those Catholic boys. It makes me want to go up front and yell 'Nietzsche killed God!' But I hold back, gather my wits, I'm stoned. We are eating their biscuits after all. God knows what they'll be thinking, what these people are capable of. *We need to get out of here.*

Stinky has finished his Superwines. Helen is drying up in the corner, getting her ear chewed off by a young grease ball in a shirt and tie, who's looking a little too excited for post Sunday mass. This seems an ideal time to gather the troops, except Hippie Pete has become fascinated by a miniature display of baby Jesus in the manger. He's got his head right up close to the figurines. The three wise men, the sheep and animals, all looking in at Mary and baby Jesus in an aura of golden tinsel. I tap him on the shoulder. "Hey, I reckon it's time we go."

"Check it out," he says.

I shrug. "Let's get out of here, man."

He shakes his head. "No, this is authentic. The real deal."

"What do you mean?"

"You see what they're all made of?"

Stinky squeezes between us. "Hey, what'ya looking at?"

We all look down, study the manger. It's clearly made by kids. The animals are plasticine, and the three wise men are basically dressed up popsicle sticks. "All I see is just the regular birth of Christ scene."

"You see what baby Jesus is made of?"

I look closer. "Is he... is that what I think it is?"

Stinky beams. "Hey, what do ya know, he's a jelly baby wrapped in tissue paper."

Hippie Pete looks at me. "You get the meaning?"

I take a stab in the dark. "Jesus is a lolly?"

"No, the embodiment of Christ is something you invite into you. You take the spirit in, ingest it. He is God's offering to the mortals."

I nod. "Yeah, I think you're overreading this one, man. You've smoked your mind. Now let's go."

"All right," he says.

We leave Stinky to take one last look at the manger while we go rescue Helen.

25

"I can't believe you ate baby Jesus!" Hippie Pete cries. "What's wrong with you?"

Stinky seems nonchalant about the whole thing, having confessed once we got back on the road. He shrugs. "It was just a jelly baby. I was hungry."

"If you had waited, I would've given you a whole bag of them. All those kids will now be wondering where the hell their saviour has gone."

"Perhaps resurrected prematurely?" I say, with tongue and cheek. I look across at Helen who's grinning.

"More like churning in the bottom of his stomach," Hippie Pete continues. "What you did may seem small, but in terms of the universe there'll be some karmic wave of retribution happening right now, a ripple effect, and I'm just hoping we're not in its path."

"Or he could have the spirit of Jesus in him, right?" I add, trying to smooth the atmosphere.

"What flavour was he?" Helen asks, smiling.

Stinky looks out the window, then after a pause, says, "Lemonade."

And again the dice are thrown into the deep cosmic corners of the van. This time at a fork in the road. Odds –

we head out towards the golden sands, or evens – we go left to Farewell Spit. There is some debate as to the angle the dice land in, but in the end it's unanimous. We're heading towards the golden sand beaches of Abel Tasman.

As we hug the Pohara coastline of looming chalk-white cliffs, two hitchhikers come into view. Stinky yells at Hippie Pete to stop. He gets such a fright he almost swerves off the road. The fact that the hitchhikers are two drop dead gorgeous blondes with backpacks, may have something to do with Stinky's overenthusiastic shrill in his voice that almost causes us to crash. Helen is rolling her eyes by the time we stop and pull over. Given we've overshot the pair, they'll likely take a little while to reach the van. "Hold on," Hippie Pete says. "We should roll the dice to decide whether we pick them up."

"You're a nut," Stinky replies. "We're not rolling on this one. Besides, it's too late."

"Not for the universe it's not. It can decide at any time it wants. And I say we go random all the way." He turns to face us. "How about it?"

Helen and I look at each other, still a little blazed as we assess the situation. The hitchhikers are seconds away. Helen sighs and does the only decent thing to do.

The hitchhikers, Anika and Ingvil, are from Sweden, both students specialising in child psychology. We learn all this as the pair sit opposite us in a spare set of fold out beach chairs. They haven't stopped smiling since they got in, maybe nervous smiles given the rudimentary seating arrangement and the pointed questions coming from

Stinky, who by all accounts looks like a runaway hobo. Hippie Pete hasn't said much, probably a little hurt we rejected his dice. The pair are of that look that is foreign in New Zealand. Hair blonder than blonde, olive skin, blue eyes and a sweet Scandinavian accent dancing over their syllables. It's no wonder they catch the eye of the average kiwi male. I try to ignore their looks, ask neutral questions, but Stinky is practically drooling, craning his neck towards them.

"So, you're planning to do the tramp?" I ask.

"Tramp?" Anika, the taller of the two, asks. "What is tramp?"

"Oh yeah, sorry I forgot. Tramping is what you might call trekking," I explain.

"Ah," she nods. "Yes, we tramp Abel Tasman. You as well?"

I shake my head. "We're just day trippers. But we can take you to the start of the track if you want."

They look at each other briefly. "We stay at, what it is called, Awanui Lodge."

"You mean Awaroa Lodge," Hippie Pete pipes up.

"Yes. You know where it is?"

He glances at the sea briefly. "You planning on getting there tonight?"

They nod. "Yes... why?"

"The tide is coming in. You need to cross soon or you won't make it."

Anika frowns. "We have to cross something?"

"Yeah, a large inlet. It can still be done. I know a short cut where you can cross lower down, but you'll have to miss the first part of the track. We can take you straight there if you want?"

They look at each other again. "It's not a problem for you?"

Stinky butts in, smiles. "No problem at all. It'll be our pleasure."

I look away, feeling a little awkward at Stinky's over eagerness. But who can blame him?

"Thank you," she says. "You kiwis are always so nice to us. Very friendly your country you have." I look out the window. Oh, I wonder, why that is? Nevertheless, I'm feeling good about today – a random harmonious quality to our journey with delightfully unexpected turns. I've almost forgotten the rest of my woes. The tar seal ends and the van hits the dirt road. We hold on as our chairs rattle and vibrate.

26

The sun is baking. Heat waves ripple along the horizon of a three-kilometre-wide inlet. From the carpark, Hippie Pete points out to the girls where they have to cross – a diagonal walk towards a bright orange marker you can just make out in the distance. "That should get you on the track from there. Awaroa Lodge is signposted from that marker." They thank us with smiles and we watch them as they begin their crossing. The water is up to their ankles to begin with, then knee deep.

"You sure they can get across?" I ask.

Hippie Pete nods. "It only goes up to waist at its deepest. But if they waited another hour the tide would be over their heads."

"Why don't we go with them?" Stinky asks.

Hippie Pete turns. "Because if we go then we're stuck there until the tide goes out, which will be about one in the morning."

Stinky beams. "Sounds fun."

"But what about food," Helen says. "We haven't got much, we'll starve."

"What about the lodge," I ask. "Do they sell food there?"

He nods. "Yeah. There's actually a restaurant and bar. Right in the middle of nowhere."

"You're kidding, right?"

"No, I'm serious. I was a woofer there last summer. It's a pretty cool set up."

"Damn," Stinky says. "If only I had some funds."

Hippie Pete nods. "Past my budget too, man."

Sensing the disappointing vibe, I do a quick inventory of my wallet. It's still pretty well stocked in blood money. Something good could come from this loot after all. "Hey, guys, I can cover it. The milky bars are on me."

It doesn't take long to catch up with the Swedes. Their faces beam when we show up. They're struggling to keep their packs above the water as they wade over waist deep. Hippie Pete has somewhat underestimated the incoming tide, but makes amends when he offers to take their backpacks for them. Stinky is all too willing to assist, so the girls happily take up their gentlemanly offer. Hippie Pete and Stinky have to lift the packs well above them, a kind of strange sight like something out of Africa as they balance some of the weight on the tops of their heads. Meanwhile, the rest of us have taken off what we don't want getting wet and bundled it above the waterline, which at its deepest is over my waist, licking at the edges of my burn dressing. The doctor instructed not to get it wet under any circumstances, but it's hard not to sense the tranquillity of this inlet. The sun warmed current against the skin, the outcries of Oystercatchers stalking across the marshland, and the squishy mud squeezing between your toes. There's a warm silence between us, or at least it lasts until we hit a bed of razor-sharp cockle shells. Helen is the first victim to curse the sky, followed by the Swedes cursing expletives in their native tongue. The boys nevertheless guide the group around the cockle beds as best they can.

We reach the other side, put our shoes on, and follow the track that leads us around a golden shoal of sand and tropical blue water. It seems so inviting with lush native bush all the way down to the water's edge. The Swedes take some photos, then we head on to the lodge where they check-in.

We're waiting for them in the garden bar. This place is like no other. No roads leading in. A standalone building nestled in the middle of the bush you can only access by foot. Hippie Pete tells us they have to boat-in supplies and carry everything from the beach. There is the sound of a generator working overtime to keep the beer cool. The place is abuzz with waiters delivering plates of food, taking orders from jaded trampers and spritely looking day trippers like us. A round of beers and a bowl of mussels arrive at our table. They're the best thing that's touched my palate in weeks. For so long I've been eating Hangdog stodge which usually equates to pasta and sauce followed by more pasta and sauce. When was the last time I ate anything fresh? And the beer, it's really cold and thirst quenching in this golden heat.

The Swedes arrive. They look... well... Stinky and Hippie Pete look a bit speechless, and if I were honest it's going to be hard to look them in the eye. I know the Scandinavians are known for their relaxed attitude when it comes to baring skin, but it still doesn't make it easy to curb your response to their bikinied bodies with an almost transparent cotton shawl wrapped around their lower half. I glance away briefly and notice Helen looking at me, as if judging my reaction. I feel uneasy all of sudden, and am somewhat annoyed I should even have to entertain the slightest pang of guilt. We're not an item. I thought I'd buried any romantic thoughts of her, but then my mind travels back to the river, the way she looked at me. To say I'm confused right now would be an understatement. I reach for my beer, gulp it down halfway. That's better. Bury and forget.

Anika and Ingvil order a bottle of white and a couple of bowls of wedges as a way of saying thanks for our guided tour. The beers keep coming, the sun beats down, and soon a lively conversation opens up with Hippie Pete regaling the jelly baby incident but with more humorous zeal now. He's had a couple of drinks and probably realises this Karmic wave of retribution may be just in his head. The girls clearly find it funny; they haven't stopped smiling each time they look at Stinky, who by all accounts doesn't appear to care that he might be the butt of a joke. He's probably thinking they fancy him. Maybe they do? Who knows what could come of this day?

27

We've migrated to the beach, our bellies full of food and beer, burying our legs in the sand and squinting out at the shimmer of cobalt blue sea. The Swedes decide it's time for a swim. They take their shawls off and walk slowly to the water's edge like in some swimwear model routine. Hippie Pete and Stinky follow shortly, all eager and limber, which leaves Helen and I alone, and there is no doubt about the electric discordant note between us that needs to be treated with care. I want to join them, hide in the water, seal my eyes and ears like in the bucket game with only the silent familiarity of my thoughts. But I can't, doctor's orders, and I have to say something or the awkwardness will increase. "So, you're not joining them?" I ask.

She shakes her head. "Nah, maybe later."

I look out at them splashing, diving and dipping like playful seals. "That water looks divine," I say. "What I'd give to dive in right now."

"When can you?" she asks.

"Oh, maybe in a week, when the dressing comes off." I sigh. "Can't wait."

Helen nods, drawing a spiral in the sand with her finger. "Do you mind if I ask why you did it?"

"Did what?"

She looks at me. "Why you jumped into the fire. What were you actually thinking?"

I shrug, somewhat uncomfortable with the whole question. I just wanted the superficial chitchat stuff; now she's drilling me about something I don't even know how to answer. "It was the booze," I say, trying to blow her off. "I do crazy shit when I'm drunk, I guess."

"Yeah, but I think everyone was wasted. But you..." She sighs. "Holy shit, Kurt. That was insane..." She looks down, continues with her spirals. "Sorry for being so nosey, but it kind of seemed you had total disregard for yourself. Like you just didn't care." She pauses. "Have you always been like that?"

God, who does she think she is, my mother? "What does it matter to you?" I say. "Why do you care all of sudden?" She looks at me, a little stunned by my reaction. *I'm a little stunned.* I'm never usually this snappy with anyone.

"I'm just worried about you, Kurt, that's all."

I pause, sigh. "Sorry... I didn't mean to... I mean..." I put my head down, feel like such a douche. She's just trying to be nice and I have to go ape at her. "I'm... well. How do I explain it? It's not like I intentionally wanted to burn myself. That wasn't part of the plan. It just seemed a great idea at the time."

Her eyes widen. "A great idea?"

"Well, it was more of a feeling I get. Like I just want to risk it all, just for the thrill of it."

She nods. "Like an adrenaline rush?"

"Yeah, but really intense. Like it overrides all logic and common sense."

"And you've been like that all your life?"

I nod. "Mostly. At least these last few years. It just excites me to do crazy shit. I don't know how else to explain it."

She stares out to sea. "What happened a few years ago?"

I turn to face her. "Pardon me?"

She looks at me directly. "You said you started getting this feeling these last few years. What happened, some kind of change in your life?"

I shake my head, trying to figure her out. "I'm sorry, Helen. I'm just trying to understand why all this interest in me all of a sudden. Like you've turned into some kind of shrink."

She returns her eyes back to the sea. "I actually saw a shrink once. In fact... I used to be pretty messed up." She looks at me. "You want to see something? I rarely show anyone, but given I'm dealing with you, I think I should."

"So, you think I'm that fucked up, huh?"

"Nope, you just remind me how reckless I was once." She unbuttons her shorts, slides them down so that she's practically sitting next to me in her undies. "Don't worry," she says. "This is purely educational."

I'm speechless. "Um... okay."

"Look." She shows me the inside of her thighs, which appear to be dotted with small white pock marks of scar tissue. My mind goes blank, I have no idea what to say. "Cigarette burns," she says. "And before you ask. Yes, they were self-inflicted." She pulls up her shorts. "So, you see, you're not the only one who's burnt themselves."

"How... why did you do that?"

Her eyes look confidently into mine. "Oh, probably for the same reason you jumped into the fire."

"But you did that on purpose, you intentionally wanted to harm yourself."

"Did I? Or was it because I wanted some kind of release, some kind of rush?"

I shake my head. "I don't know. It seems pretty different to me. I was completely drunk."

"So was I."

"Well how about the obvious?"

"And that is?" There's a long pause. Her eye contact is unwavering.

"Why you did it?"

"Oh, so we're back to that question." She sighs, looks out to the horizon. "It was years back. My parents, they had just split, and my boyfriend at the time..." She smiles sarcastically, taking a moment to recollect. "Well, I actually thought I was so in love with him. He broke it off after I found out he was cheating." She pauses for reflection. "I don't think I could ever cheat on someone, you know, not after what it felt like." She looks into my eyes, for a tender second, like what she's saying is a nice way of warning me off – *don't even go there.*

"It must have hurt," I say.

"I self-imploded, loathed myself, somehow blamed myself for him cheating. My parents, they were rolling in their own crap, so I felt I had nowhere to turn."

"And that's when you turned on yourself?"

She nods. "Drank a good half bottle of vodka." She looks down. "The rest, well, you've seen what I did."

"I'm sorry that happened," I say. "Hope you don't do that again to yourself."

"Oh, that's cute. So, it's okay for you to be concerned about me, but it's plain weird if I'm concerned that you burnt about a third of your body?"

I nod, raise my arms in surrender. "Okay. Fair cop. I allow you to be concerned."

"You've missed the point. You should be concerned for yourself. Next time you could do some real damage."

"Yeah, I suppose."

There's a long silence between us. She's called my bluff, but in a good way. I'm starting to see what she's getting at. And I'd somehow deluded myself into thinking that what I did was just antics. Perhaps I'm more unhinged than I thought. In fact, if I told her the whole truth, why I'm here, what we're running from, it would sound like madman stuff. If only she knew the half of it. But then maybe all of this is somehow linked. Jumping into the fire, hooking into Lincoln's mad plan, risking it all. My current trajectory is heading into another galaxy far far away from any orbit that could be considered on the fringe of normal. Yes, I want the thrill, but at what price?

I turn to her. "I have a hunch."

"Pardon me."

"About why I like to do crazy shit. It may be a long shot. But all I can come up with is that it might have something to do with what happened in my childhood."

"I'm all ears," she says.

"Well, I don't think it's directly related. I don't even know if it has anything to do with the way I am, given it happened so many years ago. But I'm going to say it anyway because there's nothing else to go on. In fact, I haven't ever really talked about it much." I squint at her. "You know how I told you I don't have any siblings?"

"Yeah."

"Well, I lied, kind of. I meant no siblings that are alive. I had an older brother, Leighton... but he died when he was like six years old."

She pauses. "I'm sorry to hear that."

I shrug. "There's nothing really to be sorry about. I didn't really know him. I was two at the time. I have next to no memories of him apart from photographs. I've kind of grown up as an only child despite it not starting out that way."

"How did it happen, if you don't mind me asking?"

"Hit by a car, on the way home from school. He just ran across the road blindly."

"That must have really affected your parents."

I nod. "Yeah, it must have. Probably still does... funny though..."

"Why's that?

"Well, I haven't really thought about them in that way. It seems obvious, now that you've said it out loud – them being affected and all. It must have really changed their lives radically. They didn't really talk about him much, not to me anyway. And I guess I was so caught up in my own childhood that I never asked."

"Kurt, no child would be expected to ask their parents about how they were processing their grief."

"Yeah, I know. It's just weird I haven't really thought of them as grieving adults. They're just my olds, if you know what I mean. And annoying at that. I mean, especially my mother. She's a complete control freak. Ever since I was like thirteen or fourteen when I was, you know, wanting to try stuff out and be more independent, she came down hard on me always. And I don't mean the usual curfew and rules. She never let me try anything remotely interesting, especially if it involved a smidgen of risk. Going to parties, forget it. Going wild just for a moment was near impossible."

"Give me an example?"

I nod. "Okay. You ever been swimming at a surf beach as a kid?"

"Yeah, heaps of times."

I shake my head. "Me, not once. My mother forbade me to even go near the water's edge, even between the flags. I was allowed to play in the sand, but that was it, on the proviso I wore floaties on my arms. She was fanatical with safety. She thought some gigantic wave was going to sweep me away anytime. So, you can imagine how she was as I grew older. Yes, I was allowed to go to the school ball, but not the after function, AKA where all the actual fun happens. Even during school, in phys ed, I was forbidden to play rugby – I had a special exemption letter sent from my beloved mum. You have any idea how lame it felt standing on the side line, being singled out as only allowed to watch? She was the lead campaigner for banning full contact bull-rush during the school lunch hour. I was never allowed to skateboard or surf or do anything 'fun'. To say she was a killjoy, would be an understatement."

"Jeez, how did you cope?"

"Oh, I had ways, when she wasn't around. Like in the lunch hour at school I scaled trees, all the way to the top. And I'd do other stunts, like climb up on the school roof when a ball got stuck up there, or sneak out of bounds to the golf course and try to steal golf balls straight off the greens. Just to feel free and reckless for a second."

Helen nods. "That makes sense. Kind of puts your 'jumping in the fire' in context."

"How do you mean?"

She looks at me, a little wide eyed. "You don't see how your brother's death meant your mother lived in fear, probably still does, that something similar might happen to you?"

"Yeah, I guess you could see it that way."

"Kurt, I mean she obviously tried to do everything in her power to prevent you from harm, even though you saw it as her just being controlling. It's no wonder you like doing crazy stuff. You identify freedom with doing risky dangerous shit, when most would settle for something less extreme."

I smile somewhat nervously, knowing she's pretty much hit the nail. I want to refute it but there is nothing I can say right now that would make more sense than what she has just said. "Well, I… I don't have any comeback to that." I take a deep breath, exhale the truth I have always evaded. It's out in the open, and with this I feel a little lighter, able to see it for what it is, now that it's been extracted from the subconscious. Jumping into the fire, deciding to go along on this crazy ride, all my reckless decisions, all stem from one psychological thread inside my head pulling me towards danger. The problem now, how do I turn back when I'm up to my neck in badass? "Okay, you're completely right," I say. "You're good. Forget teaching. You should be a psychologist or something."

She laughs it off. "You're just saying that."

"I'm serious. You're a natural. You should look into it."

She smiles, and those cute dimples appear. "I'll take it as a compliment," she says.

The lightness I'm feeling gives me a surge of confidence. I take another deep breath, exhale. "I've been meaning to ask you something."

She flicks her hair to the side. "Oh yeah, what's that?"

I'm about to start when we notice the others coming out of the water. "Want to take a walk?"

She nods. "Yeah, sure."

The sand is so dry it squeaks under our feet, and the bright green off the sea gives it that emerald quality. Some time passes before I rebuild my confidence. "You know that time when you got stuck in the river?"

She smiles at her feet. "Oh... I was wondering when you were going to bring that up."

"Yeah... um..."

She looks at me, "I know... I've been thinking about that as well."

"You have?"

"Yeah, I've been trying to work out what to say in case you asked me about it. And now that you're asking, I still haven't really got an answer that'll make a lot of sense."

I nod, grin. "Don't worry. You can try it on me first, for practice."

She laughs. "Sure, sounds easy." She pauses. "Well, I'm going to be honest with you, since this is honesty hour." She looks away momentarily to gather her thoughts. "I'm embarrassed when it comes down to it. Maybe even disappointed in myself. Not that anything happened, thank God. Just that, you know..."

I wonder if she's noticing my cheeks going red, because I can certainly feel them. I nod, laugh nervously, "Yeah, that would have been a little awkward if something did happen, I guess." This is followed by an unwanted silence. I swallow. "Um... did you... like... want something to happen, by any chance?" *God, now I sound desperate.*

"Then or now?"

I smile, shrug. "Um... both?"

She sighs. "I like you, Kurt. And maybe under different circumstances I might have wanted something to happen, but you know how I felt when someone cheated on me, so why would I want to inflict that on someone else?"

I nod. "You're right."

"I mean... I think its pretty bold of you to ask. Most guys don't come right out and say stuff like that. Usually they just act weird around me."

"Really?"

"Yeah, really. I like that about you."

I pause. "Actually, normally I do the 'act weird around girls' routine. I'm still learning. That's just a one-off, I'm afraid."

She smiles, looks warmly into my eyes. "Well, you should keep doing it. It suits you." She stops. "So, that's all you wanted to talk about then?"

I nod, hesitate for a moment. "Yeah, I think that's about all of it."

28

After a whole day of sun, bar and beach we say our farewells to the Swedes at midnight. Guided by the light of a near full moon, it's a silent, peaceful walk across the inlet which seems like a world of small popping sounds as crabs blow bubbles in the mud. No one says much to anyone. There's a tired focus amongst us to just get back to the van and back to Hangdog.

We sleep in, all of us, and rise late morning to tell Lincoln about our adventure. He nods, appears to listen but not really, as he's busy shaving his legs. He seems a little distant from the group. Or maybe he seems different to me now. Before it seemed like we were a duo, bearing a secret, whereas now he's just a sore reminder of my predicament.

For the next couple of days, I keep thinking how I got to this point, fuelled by my desire for danger, only to now apply the brakes and find there's no slowing down or turning back. I open my mind to the big question of my involvement. I know why Lincoln is here. This leaves the burning question: *Do I really need to be here?* I remain anonymous after all. Lincoln is my only connection to the money. I know why I chose to stick with him, only that it's based on what he's telling me, and how do I know he's not pulling the wool? Maybe he's made all this stuff up about Hohepa? Maybe he's not that bad. Maybe it would be convenient to fabricate a story about some crazed monster if all you want is for the other person to believe that sticking around is better than splitting with their share of the money. He wants it all to himself, I'm thinking. It's plausible.

This morning I have a cunning plan. I've written a note, using block capitals to disguise my handwriting, and attached it to the fly of the tent. The others are out on the ford climbing. Lincoln's gone for a swim and will be back shortly. I'm sipping stovetop espresso, reclining in the hammock with a book, when Lincoln returns and hangs his towel in the trees. He sees the note pretty much straightaway. I'm pretending to read while he picks up the note. He's staring at it intensely. I'm presuming he's re-reading it a number of times to make sure of what it's actually saying. His face takes on a deathly white pallor; he darts his head around, hyper alert. "Fuck!" he says.

I look up. "What is it?"

"When did this note arrive?"

I shrug. "I don't know."

"You've been here all this time, right?"

"Kinda. What's this about?"

Panic sets in. "We've got to go!"

"What do you mean, we've got to go? Where are we going?"

"Getting out of here, is what. Pack your things." He pauses. "Wait. No, leave everything as it is. He'll think we haven't gone. Get in the car, we're leaving!" He goes to grab the keys, but I'm not moving, enjoying this little escapade. "Who's he?"

"Hohepa, for fucksake. It's on the note from Sid. He's been here, enquiring about us, maybe a few minutes ago. Now, get in the car!" He hops in the driver's seat, starts the engine.

I shake my head. "No," I say. "I'm staying put. I want out. I want my share."

"You fucking what?"

I stand my ground. "You heard me."

"Okay, whatever," he says. "If that's the way you want it." He gets out and opens the rear door and starts to pry open the inner casing. Part of me now is thinking I should just let him go, be done with it. Hell, I could even let him take all the money. He's been nothing but a thorn in my side, and I've been riding his directionless wave of destruction with no end in sight. But then again, I can't see the future, blinded by uncertainty and the gut feeling Lincoln could be right about all of this. Maybe sticking together, for the interim anyway, is the only way out. In fact, the only thing I *can* be certain about is that if he gets caught by Hohepa he won't spare a moment without blabbing about me.

"Sit down, Lincoln, relax. It's bogus."

He looks at me, puzzled. "What?"

I sigh and look away. "I wrote the note."

He clicks the casing back on. "You fucking what?"

"I fabricated the whole thing." I pause. "To see what your reaction would be."

He stands and starts pacing, clearly pissed. "Why the fuck would you do that? Shit, fucking shit, you bastard!"

"Look," I say. "I'm sorry, I just needed to know where you truly stood. I mean, there's a lot at stake. Not only the cash, but also my life. You understand?"

He stops pacing, he's calmed a little. "You thought I was bullshitting?"

"Put it this way. It's not about trust. I would do the same to anyone if I've only known them for a few months. Wouldn't you?" *I'm totally lying.*

"Whatever," he says, and sits down. "You really fucking had me. I was shitting bricks."

"You really need me on this, don't you?"

He pauses before answering. "Listen, if you think this is about money you haven't understood one bloody thing. This is survival."

I nod. "I know that now. But one question: where to next? There's nowhere in this country he won't be able to track us down. It just seems we're waiting on borrowed time. We need to come up with an exit plan?"

He nods, stares into thin air. "Yup."

29

The next day I hitch into Takaka to see the doc. This is my fourth visit since jumping into the fire. Each time he comments how well the skin is regenerating. Today the bandage and the fishnet comes off and all that remains is a dry pad to keep it clean, which he reckons I can remove in a couple of days and just let it breathe. I like that idea – breathe – and the cold splash of water on my back. The doc reckons I may not even get permanent scarring. I'm relieved, and can't help but think this is like a second chance or second skin.

After my appointment, I check my emails and I'm surprised to see a message from my mother. She's forgiven me, it seems. She wants me back home for Christmas, from wherever I am, flights paid for. Suddenly I'm homesick, followed by a rush of guilt.

Homesickness. I'm almost embarrassed by the thought. I'd imagined being stronger, more resilient, especially when I know the days spent up there will be fuelled by arguing and misunderstanding and intergenerational warfare. I would need a team of expert diplomats trained in terrorist negotiations to avoid an argument with my mother. Nevertheless, that's what I miss

– arguing with someone who actually cares. Someone who can tell me what to do with my life, since right now, I haven't a clue.

But now is not the time to go up there. Dragging them into my problem is the last thing I want. Besides, I can see exactly how Christmas day will pan out, like every other Christmas day in the past few years. The order of events, timing, what we'll eat and the conversations we'll have will be the same, only that when we go for the afternoon beach swim I won't jump in, for the reason of having to explain the healing scar on my back. They'll be yelling at me from the water, telling me how warm it is. I'll be sitting on the sand, shaking my head, telling them it looks cold. Of course, I'll want to be in there with them. Cheltenham beach is where I grew up. Devonport – I couldn't have asked for a better place to spend my childhood. I'm lucky. My mother, for all her failings, bent over backwards to give me the best start. Her overbearing control was based on fear of losing me, and if that's how she shows her love, then that's how it is. If anything happens to me, and they ask themselves what they did wrong, I would say absolutely nothing. The mess I'm in is completely my own.

For a brief moment, I envision watching my parents from the beach as they swim out. I'm conscious they're moving away as I sit, stationary, drawing circles in the sand.

30

Christmas Day in scumbag corner went something like this: Stinky tried to bake a cake in a frying pan. There was an attempt at doing a hangi, but with no one experienced in the culinary method we basically buried our food for a couple of hours before pulling it out raw. The only success was Helen making a batch of chocolate vodka.

Then, on the morning after Boxing Day, a team of police swooped into Hangdog. Hippie Pete thought immediately about his stash of weed. Lincoln made himself scarce. But the warrant was for some person named Peter McCallum. We stared blankly at each other and were slow to twig until Stinky emerged from under his tarp.

A few days later I'm sitting in the Wholemeal Café with a newspaper, sipping an organic beer, reading about it. After his arrest, rumours spread through the camp he'd been on the run for weeks. Hard to believe, Stinky – a fugitive and now technically famous. A whole page spread in the *Herald* tells you all about it. A couple of months ago, on route between Nelson District Court and remand prison, there was a breakout of a prisoner security van – two others and Stinky (or Peter McCallum as the article identifies him as). Stinky was only on remand for a relatively minor charge whereas the other two, who orchestrated the escape, were looking at lengthy prison sentences. Instant freedom must have flowed through his mind and he took it. He's smiling in the picture, an urban scene, the last to be caught, handcuffed with police on either side as he's taken into custody. So much for the mystery shrouding Stinky. So long and farewell.

I take a sip of beer, leaf through the paper and stop at an article about The Gathering. As I read through, it adds to my excitement knowing it's New Year's Eve tonight and that right now people from all parts of the country and overseas will be arriving at the base of Takaka Hill, in the Cobb Valley. The Gathering, or G1 as they're calling it, is expected to attract over ten thousand people, culminating in a three day dance event: One hundred and eighty DJs, seven dance zones, eighty-two live acts, including Pitch Black, Way Out West, Trinity, Shapeshifter, Salmonella Dub, Clinton Smiley, Delray System, King Kapisi, The Nomad, Chris Knox, The Dance Hall Dons, Storm and Digital and many more… a seventy-two hour, alcohol-free dance festival, fuelled by drugs and the stampede of a thousand hippie feet. This party is forecast to be the biggest ever. From humble beginnings in the early nineties, Entrain – a group of locals colluding on Takaka Hill for a non-profit good time dancing their little hearts out – drew larger crowds each year and spawned the first Gathering in 1996. Since then it has grown into a dance

Mecca, steadily increasing in numbers and becoming known internationally as a serious party destination. Last year it rained for three days and the Canaan Downs area turned into a giant mud bath, breeding hypothermic tripped out mutants caked in mud. This completely destroyed the grounds, hence the change of site to the Cobb.

The article digs deeper into the hype surrounding The Gathering this year; a mixed review about police concern around the drug scene versus the impeccable history of a non-violent, alcohol free event and a chance offering of bringing humanity together. The organisers claim they are still holding onto the principles of Entrain, but as ticket sales soar and more money is being made, it appears those principles may only be holding by a fiscal thread. There's a real fear that the change in site and the profiteering angle may contaminate the spirit of The Gathering. I'm hoping this is not the case. I've never been, only heard a lot about it and seen the enchanted look on those who have experienced it.

I flick back to the picture of Stinky to take one last look before I leave. Inset is a smaller photo I hadn't noticed before – taken of Hangdog and a mention of where he's been hiding all this time. It's a shot of the entrance taken from the road. There are two figures walking down the gravel drive, climbing gear slung over their shoulders. A wave of nerves hit. I inch closer... then closer. It's definitely *them*. Lincoln and Helen. Is he actually identifiable, noticeable to someone who might want to know his whereabouts? His face is grainy and the only way

I can make out it's him is his unmistakable white toothed grin. He's looking down slightly, unaware of the photographer. I put the paper down, hold my face in my hands, breathe in deeply. I sit up with a sigh and take another look at the photo. This time I feel a tad better. The only reason I noticed the article in the first place was because I saw Stinky, not Lincoln. Hohepa won't know Stinky, or there is a good chance he doesn't, so he won't have any motive to pry further into the photo, if he ever reads the newspaper to begin with. The probability of Lincoln being identified and associated with Hangdog is so slim I'm convinced it's almost a non-issue. Why even mention it to Lincoln? Besides, if I tell him he'll go ape and want to leave and I'll miss out on the biggest party ever. I close the paper, tuck it under the magazine rack, and finish the dregs of my beer.

31

I can see the masses of tents already dotted at the mouth of the Cobb Valley, and a shimmering line of slow-moving traffic stretched along a narrow road from the entrance. Soon we arrive at the tail end of that queue – Hippie Pete, Helen, Lincoln, me – all brimming with excitement as the Skoda nudges forward.

Twenty minutes and we're at the gate. Security are checking tickets and searching cars for alcohol, and they're finding it too. There's a large caged trailer, already half full of confiscated booze. Rumour has it the event staff get together each year after the party is over and have a huge piss up on the confiscated liquor. A nice gesture for their hard work and clear motivation to search the vehicles thoroughly.

We're processed through with yellow bands clamped to our wrists, tagged like some special breed of cattle. The air is alive with invisible wires connecting every soul who's come to dance and sweat their minds away for the next seventy-two hours. The dance zones haven't opened yet, thousands of tents and thousands of people swarming in this paddock, planning their itinerary on the buffet of sound almost upon them. For every second person there's a smile, and for every other they'll soon be smiling if they haven't dropped already. Some walk by in costume; fluorescent, multi-coloured clothes and hats and sparkling green aliens on stilts. I get the feeling I'm behind the scenes, behind the curtains, enmeshed in a rehearsal of what's about to hit centre stage.

Weaving amongst the massive area of tents we drive into an empty space and make camp.

The dance zones open at two in the afternoon. A flood of people converges on the twenty minute hike along a narrow road, following the river up into a large cul-de-sac plateau surrounded by steep, bush clad hills. I can see why they chose this area – a natural amphitheatre locking in the sound.

We're drawn instinctively to the trance zone – the grand epicentre of the party that will cater to thousands of jumping bodies on the stroke of midnight. The zone is marked out by large bone white posts, bent inwards, mimicking the skeleton of some whale or mammoth creature. There's already a mass of serious ravers leaping and throwing their bodies around. We try to join in, but we merely get a groove on, clearly undernourished of major party drugs. Marijuana is not cutting enough to spark the wild dance in me yet, especially in raw daylight. We resign to the periphery of the crowd, looking in at those who have pushed their pills early.

We discuss our drug plan, because everyone needs a drug plan when you're armed to the teeth. There's consensus on taking ecstasy tonight, LSD tomorrow, and smoking enough weed to enhance the potential of both these drugs. I've been handed a pamphlet by the organisers – information on safe drug taking at The Gathering. Advice includes: always stay hydrated and have a tripping buddy on hand; take half of whatever you're taking if unsure of dose strength; and if it all gets super weird then there is the safe tent on standby ready to receive you. It all seems a refreshing change from a society usually warning you not to take drugs, ever.

We sample the other zones: Hardcore, House, Ambience, Tribal. The sun is going down, the zones are filling but not many people are dancing yet, no doubt saving themselves for tonight. We agree to head back, eat and hydrate, and return at dusk.

32

We're in the House tent finding our groove. What began as four of us in a closed circle is now broken, inviting strangers into our dance, and we're smiling indiscriminately at the social mass grooving all around us. The floor is covered with straw, giving off a fresh barn smell. The air is starting to sweat from all the body heat. What I'm feeling from the ecstasy is intensifying. I try to confer with Lincoln, given this is my first time on E. I yell over the music, "I'm getting a good vibe!"

He's smiling, nodding. "Yeah, man. You're on the way!"

"To where?"

"You'll see!" He grins and veers off into the crowd to find Helen who's momentarily disappeared. Hippie Pete, barefooted and kitted out in bright orange fisherman pants, is really pulling out the moves. What used to be his seemingly permanent smile has now completely taken over his face, twisting it into that of some deranged Buddha. Everywhere I look there's an unusual number of cowboy hats, all nodding in time to the beat. There is even an Elvis in a sparkly flared costume, thick mutton chops, moving in soulful groove, possessed by the spirit of why we're all here. I'm a part of this music, it seems, this tent, these people I feel strangely connected to. Every person around me, I'm convinced, is tuned to the same frequency of neural pleasure.

Is this the peak? Because I've never loved a crowd, really truly adored every person dancing, beating to the rhythm of a collective heart. It appears I've lost everyone, but it doesn't matter as I drift into a group of shirtless guys with cowboy hats, glistening chests, smiling at me, knowing we are all part of something whole, totally, inexplicably it seems, and there's not a moment of hesitation that they might be gay or that it matters as one of them moves in to massage my shoulders. I let him. It feels completely right, the most natural thing in the world to have another man, who you barely know, massage you in public, because what I'm getting is warm shudders coating over me in layers of sweet liquid rush. Oh joy and inhalation of this beautiful drug. I'm thinking maybe, just maybe, it's more than the drug – that this is the essence of what I've come here for, that what's happening to me is real. When is this massage going to end? Christ, perhaps he wants me to reciprocate? I turn around and there is simply no one there, yet the feeling remains all over my body – this has to be the peak. My God, my brain is going to ejaculate.

But I hold on, follow the exodus of people heading to the Trance zone for the countdown. A minute before midnight – Pitch Black are on stage synthesising an orchestra of sound pulsing through the crowd. The night air is cut with lasers, and with the dry smoke rising off the sea of heads a thin vapour hangs over us – an alien atmosphere I put my hand through, poking my fingers playfully to the other side – then it curves and begins to rotate, spinning faster and faster with a blistering show of strobes and reverberating base thronging, every soul counting down to zero. The Scumbags are elsewhere but I'm not alone, jumping and leaping with this seething mass of people. Fireworks, smoke machines, a crescendo rise in the music and we all release our load.

I dance and dance, squeezing every last drop of this neural nectar. But after an hour there is a noticeable slide in the warmth of this crowd. For a moment I think it's them – they've changed – only to realise sadly the finite capacity of this wonderful drug.

With a bit of zone hopping I find the others in the Happy Hardcore tent – an intense strobe blend of death metal and drum 'n' base. I hit up Lincoln for some weed and he produces a joint from a container packed full of them, pre-rolled. The smoke gives some lift, slows the come down, but I have to be at it constantly every half hour, stoning up, enhancing what life remains of this great chemical romance slipping through my fingers. I'm holding on to her petticoat, by the fingertips it seems, as my dancing slows into a swaying hobble on sunrise. Just the sun itself, all natural and golden, rising over the valley, lifts the vibe for another hour before I decide to head in.

33

A bit of hydrating and a bite of a falafel kebab sees me sitting outside the tent in full daylight. There's not much sleeping going on anywhere, just a lot of people pacing and mingling, engaging in miniature post mortems of last night, kicking a hacky sack around and hitting the never-ending bongo drum. There is no rest, it seems; this is only the beginning and everyone knows it, maybe coming down for now but not for long. We're a party in purgatory, a generation waiting for that next chemical connection.

The others return and Lincoln seems more wired than he was a few hours ago. "Let's go swimming," he suggests. "There's a crowd down by the river."

We bring along ice creams and bags of sweets and sit on the sun-warmed stones, watching bathers splash and dive into the water. I whip off my shirt and plunge in with just my gruds, but it becomes quickly apparent that I might have overdressed. A group of girls run in topless and then more girls are doing the same but completely starkers. I'm wearing tinted shades – my eyes can't help but look. Then I remind myself they're only naked women after all. If you glare too hard you only turn them into stone.

We stay awake all day and roam, sampling dance zones and food tents, loading our heads with weed. As the evening encroaches, we're sitting in the Chill Out tent, reclining on large cushions and sipping chai on low-to-the-ground tables. The DJ is playing psychedelic lounge you can't help but feel completely at ease with, watching his long Rastafarian dreads sway below his knees. I would be happy just doing this for a while, except that Lincoln calls us for an urgent meeting.

"Listen up, guys. It's time to drop."

He produces four tabs of acid and starts dropping them on our tongues. Then he gets to me. "Wait a minute," I say, looking at the small multi-coloured square he's about to pop in. "How strong is this stuff. Maybe I should take half?"

"Don't worry," Helen remarks. "It'll be fine, we'll just stick together, no matter what."

I've never had a bad trip, but I recall a friend once who had such a nightmare he ended up in a psych ward. It was like being tortured, he told me. He was discharged a couple of weeks later and swore he'd never touch the stuff again.

"Look," Lincoln says. "I'm not halving the goddamn thing, okay. It's all or nothing."

"Talk about peer pressure." I open my mouth obediently.

34

Darkness has fallen on The Gathering. We're back in the House Tent, but it's got a different vibe from last night. Fewer cowboy hats, more of an intense groove, slightly jaded, or forced like we're searching for that long lost connection. It's been two hours since we dropped and I'm feeling the first wave of heat. Then comes the trip smile – a pasted-on grin plastered to your face. With the second wave I get a nice glowing warmth, although no visuals yet. Lincoln suggests we hit the bong, get them coming on. Outside the tent, after just one toke, it's definitely changing. The heat waves rush in quick succession and I'm fully through the door, stepping into another space, a different version of the world where people walk by in clothes that appear brittle, made of candy perhaps; their faces have a wax like sheen – a festival of Madame Tussauds models, only moving, dancing. I'm amused and comfortable so far. What perplexes me, though, is that the last trip wasn't as strong at the beginning. This may be the peak, I could go a bit further but no more – this is just right.

My heart's racing. I turn to Lincoln. "Fuck, man. That pot definitely got things in motion. Can you feel it?"

Lincoln shakes his head. "Nothing much yet. I just feel stoned." Hippie Pete and Helen confess they feel something but not to the extent where I'm at.

"I'm going dancing," I tell them. I turn in the direction of the House tent, I'm walking towards the tent, then I'm standing right back where I started, like I never left. "What did you say?" Helen asks.

I'm not sure what just happened. "Hey, did I just leave you guys a second ago?"

They look at me weirdly. "You're really on the way, aren't you?" Lincoln says.

I feel flushed, anxious. "Just answer the damn question. Did I, or did I not walk away from you guys a moment ago?"

Lincoln laughs, but it's not the normal type of laughter – it decreases in volume even though I can see he's really laughing hard. Hippie Pete is saying something; he looks concerned although his lips aren't moving. "What did you just say?" I ask.

He shakes his head. "Nothing, dude. I wasn't saying anything."

Helen interjects. "Hey, guys, I think it's really coming on for me." She runs her fingers through her hair. "Far out, it's coming on strong. Let's dance."

I try to follow them back to the House tent, only I'm having some difficulty as if I'm slowing down involuntarily. I glance at my legs; they're covered in grass. I try to shake the stuff off but it seems to be growing up my thighs, consuming my entire torso. It's just the drugs,

I tell myself. You can walk, just try. But I can't and people pass me by. Are they laughing at me? What are they thinking? That I'm some retard who can't walk all of a sudden? Someone comes right up close to my ear and says something incomprehensible and walks away. Another person does the same except when I look there's no one there. Christ, I'm hearing voices. Jesus, what next? This has to be the peak. I still can't move. Hippie Pete returns. "Come on, dude. Don't just stand there, come and dance. It's the best thing for acid, stops the introspection."

"I can't," I say.

He frowns. "Of course you can dance. I've seen you."

"I mean, I can't move." I pause. "I've been turned into grass."

Hippie Pete laughs. "You what?"

"It's not funny. I'm seriously stuck, man. You need to help me."

"All right, all right." He takes me by the hand, starts pulling. "Just walk."

"I can't."

He pulls harder and I go flat on my face, feeling the grass taking me further into itself. Hippie Pete shakes me, tries to haul me to my feet but fails miserably. He goes to get the others.

"On the count of three," Lincoln says. "One, two, and..." I'm lifted into a vertical position. I look down – I'm not grass any more, instead I'm a goddamn post. "Now walk," says Lincoln. "You're not grass, you have legs."

"Well, I still can't... I'm, well... I'm a fence post."

"What the fuck?"

"Don't let go of me," I plead. "Whatever you do, don't let go!"

They all let go.

I don't fall, thank God, just stand there upright, stiff. "Now, walk. You can do it. Think baby steps," Lincoln says.

"I'm trying. My legs don't work."

He sighs. "Christ, let's just leave him here. He'll walk eventually."

"Kurt," Helen says. "Can you move your toes?"

I nod.

"Good. Now, try to move your foot, and at the same time think about this fact – fence posts don't have toes."

Magic. Cured. A key unlocks and I step out, freed. "I can walk. Fucking yes. I can actually walk, look at me!" I start jumping up and down, then the feeling returns and I try fighting it. "Kurt," Helen says, "just go with it, relax. Come and dance." She takes me by the hand. Lincoln shakes his head.

I'm now dancing, kind of. I know what I have to do to appear to be dancing – bend my knees, wave my arms, groove my hips, although I can't get the rhythm, as if the music is some kind of unattainable medium. It's just background noise that everyone here thinks is great except me. I'm trying my best to fit in, trying to mimic Hippie Pete by studying his dance moves. It all feels wrong and there's an increasing disconnection as a tidal wave of anxiety seizes my mind, dragging it back into the room, but not the same room as before – everywhere around there are people dancing in two dimensional forms. There is no thickness to their bodies, they're just flat pieces of paper – human cut outs, wobbling and contorting. Lincoln turns sideways and disappears, only to reappear as he turns again. I'm surrounded by hundreds of cubist faces – eyes and noses squashed flat. Hippie Pete begins to ripple, his body turns paper thin, transparent in parts, until I notice his limbs ripping away as if they're made of tissue paper. He's beyond rescue, and so is the crowd turning slowly into superficial layers, rippling like ribbons anchored to the ground. I can't stomach this – it's too much. Stop the bus! I hoof it out of the tent and into the cool body of the night.

Drink water. That's what I need to do. Ignore the insanity, it's no good staring at it. Think H2O, hydration, focus, get a grip. There's a drink station just outside with a queue, and this chick serving looks relatively normal and unchanging so far. *Just walk over there,* I tell myself. *Ask for a bottle of water. It's easy.*

After an anxious wait in line focusing on normal thoughts, normal things, normal everything, it's my turn to face her. "Who's next?" she says.

I know what to ask for, though I can't seem to form the words. I'm staring at her, she's staring back smiling. She appears to be mulling me over, probably suspecting something trippy is going on. "You want a bottle of water?" she asks, and slides a pump bottle in front of me. "That's three bucks." I reach down to my wallet – I only have a twenty-dollar bill, shit. When I look up to give her the note, she's not really herself any more. A demon version of her stands there with white necrotic skin, and eyes filled with a terrible green. I grab the bottle, slap down the twenty, and run.

It's a long run to gain a few metres and I stop just on the perimeter of the dance zones. No one's following. I'm alone in the dark and I have no wish to return. The last thing I need in my condition is masses of two-dimensional people, strobe lights, noise, demons selling me water. Being alone is good for now, away from all the humdrum. Maybe I should go to that safety tent? Christ, they might think I'm mental and have me locked up. No, better to stay alone. Deal with it.

I begin my walk back along the road, entertaining the idea of stopping by in the Chill Out zone, anything that might help. I lift the water bottle to my lips, forgetting for a second how to drink. Am I drinking? Not sure. The bottle is tilted and I have my lips sealed over the nipple. What next? I'm sucking on it, but the water doesn't seem to be filling my mouth. I think I need to squeeze. There's the crackling plastic sound from gripping the bottle, however it's not the bottle that is being squeezed, it's my skull, I can feel it collapse under the force of a large hand squeezing hard across my temples. I release the grip of the bottle and my head cracks back into place. Holy shit fuck! Not only is this terrifying and completely nuts, I'm starting to think I have no control over my body. I'm walking, yes, I know this, although looking down at my legs it seems they are under someone else's control. I try to stop, tell my brain to stop those legs, but they seem to be ignoring me, going forth one step after another. I've lost the helm, they are on their own course, disconnected from my brain. These arms, they don't seem a part of me either, nor my face and mouth and eyes. There is simply no mass to me that I can account for – a disturbing weightless separation drifting higher until I'm looking down just over my shoulder, slightly left of centre, not even inside my head any more. My body is walking away and my thoughts warp and delaminate from the mind's hull. Mayday... mayday... abandoning ship. I'm losing myself. I'm losing grip. There it goes.

My body walks for a while and stops, stands motionless, head cocked listening for something coming from the trees. It steps off the road, cutting into flax and ferns, brushing past Manuka, tripping over knotted roots. There's a glow of flickering light through the branches and my body gravitates to that light, stopping at the edge of a small clearing where there stands a dark shadow of a figure on the opposite side, his back turned, prodding a stick into a fire, and at the heart of the flames are stones glowing red hot. The body seems fearless. I yell at my body, scream at it to run, but not a sound exits the mouth – sealed off by its own slavery.

The man throws the stick into the fire, turns around slowly. The planet of Saturn turns on its orbital path as he faces my visiting body. "Come," he says. "Come and sit with me." He sits down on a fallen tree. My body obliges, sits next to him. He puts his arm around the body, pulls it in tightly. "Hey, good to finally catch up with you."

A few feet away is a freshly dug hole – rectangular in shape, a body's length. He stands, patting the body on the head like a dog, walks over to a spade and uses it to flatten out the fire, spreading the embers and shovelling hot stones tumbling into the hole with soft earthly thuds. He stabs the spade into a mound of dirt, then looks at the body.

"You ever had a hangi before?" He grins, rubs his hands. "Come," he says. "Come over here. I want to show you something." My body obeys – an empty husk, a future cadaver, walking up to the edge of the hole. "Your future is in there, boy. But I guess you already know that." He laughs, pushes the body, just enough to get it off balance, and the body falls, fingernails scraping the sides of the earth, the bottom sinking deeper and deeper. I'm waiting for the burning stones, the singed nerves and pain within pain. The square opening to the sky narrows above, and his grin shrinks to a small sickle moon until all there is to grope for is darkness and dirt.

35

The first thing I reconnect with is the sensation of breathing. I focus on my chest rising, falling, become aware of my limbs, aware that I'm not outside myself but centred back in my skull. I take to the water bottle, moistening my dry ordinary mouth. I spit out bits of dirt and wonder with some relief whether I'm just lost in a forest and it's dark and hopefully there's a way back.

I stumble onto tar seal, feel it grip under my shoes, and the starry night opens above and I sense control returning to my legs. As the light from the food stalls glow heavenly bright, I notice my clothes covered with smears of mud and wet pine needles. What the hell have I been doing? I study my watch. It's been three hours since I dropped the acid. Seems like days of hallucinatory memory crammed in. I'm over the hump now, thank Christ. The crest of the LSD wave finally broken.

I pass the food stalls and enter the Chill Out tent, reclining on large flat cushions, running my fingers through my hair – really feeling the physical sense of myself and relief that I haven't died or disappeared or been thrown into eternal madness. It's wonderful reuniting with my body – these hands, fingers, these legs that I can see and move and which serve such an astounding purpose. Never again am I going to take my legs for granted.

The repetitive thud reverberating up the valley makes it impossible to sleep. By the second sunrise I'm over it, wired, coming down off two nights of chemicals and not a wink. I want to leave. There's not a part of me that wants to stay. The others aren't back yet. I haven't the energy or will to think about anything else other than to get away from here, away from the noise and people and endless hum of ecstatic buzz that continually wants you.

36

A twenty-minute hitch and I'm back in the tranquillity of Hangdog. Climbers relaxing, talking quietly amongst themselves in the shade of the trees. Nothing's changed – a regular vibe that expects nothing from you – the perfect space to recover and still your broken mind.

I spend the day in the hammock, dozing, hydrating and taking long cool dips in the river. There's something calming and therapeutic about the weightlessness of being completely submerged under water, hearing the gentle click of pebbles churned by the current. A welcoming antidote to the trauma of last night, returning to the exquisite fabric of normality.

Later that afternoon Helen arrives with the Skoda. She drives in at pace and swings into Scumbag. She's alone and clearly pissed off about something.

I look up casually from the hammock. "Hey, what's up? Where are the others?"

She doesn't answer, ignores me, pulls her stuff from the car including the tent – a loose scrunched up ball as if taken down in a hurry. "You all right?" I ask.

"No," she says. "That prick!" She bites her lip, sits down at the picnic table, runs her fingers through her hair, frantically, as if infested with lice. I'm assuming 'prick' equates to Lincoln. "So, what did he do?"

She turns to me, red faced and teary. "What did he not do, is more to the point."

"You guys have an argument?"

She shakes her head. "He doesn't even know I've left." She pauses, laughs. "And I actually thought he gave a shit." Her eyes well up, there's a slight tremor in her voice. "I can't believe he would do that, right in front of me."

I already suspect what's occurred but ask anyway. "What happened?"

She stands, begins pacing. "He cheated on me. And I saw him too, getting into her tent, like he wasn't even trying to hide it." She pauses to ponder something then gets back into the car.

I pry myself out of the hammock. "Hey, wait a minute. Where're you going?" She starts the engine, reverses all the way to the main road, grinds it into gear and careers off in the direction of Takaka. And there she goes, with all her hurt and anguish. I can imagine all her old scars opening up. I should have said something to comfort her. At least offer a sympathetic ear, but all that is too late, and besides she probably just wants to be on her own for a while. I'm just hoping she doesn't revert to her old self-destructive ways. There goes our loot too. Weird, I don't even feel that concerned for the money. I lie back in the hammock and reassure myself with the thought: I just want to be here, in this sanctuary of Hangdog. I'm sure Helen will be back. She's left all her stuff behind.

37

It's getting dark. Helen's not back yet. Lincoln arrives, having got a hitch. "Where is she?"

"You mean, where is the car?"

Lincoln looks around, realises and goes into flight mode. "Tell me she hasn't left with the Skoda?"

"She left with the Skoda."

"Fuck. Fuckity fuck!" He bends down, containing his anger just enough to ask, "Where did she go?"

I shrug. "I have no idea. She told me she was pissed off at you, and took off."

"Why didn't you stop her?"

"What was I supposed to do? Restrain her, jump on the bonnet? Anyway, I'm sure she'll be back. She left her stuff."

Lincoln simmers down as he eyes her belongings. "Well, I fucking hope so. For both our sakes."

"Where's Hippie Pete?"

He shrugs. "I dunno. Still dancing, tripping somewhere."

I spend the night in the hammock, sink into a long deep sleep and wake the next morning with a pretty clear head.

Maybe a fringe of fog but nothing strong coffee can't fix. Helen isn't back and neither is the car. Lincoln tells me he hasn't slept at all.

Late morning Helen strolls into Scumbag; her body language is surprisingly relaxed as she bends calmly to collect her belongings.

"Where's the car?" Lincoln asks, tersely.

She throws her bag over her shoulders. "I'm leaving," she says.

Lincoln shrugs. "I don't care. I just want to know where my car is." He pauses. "So where is it?"

She smiles, beaming smugness. "I think you're meaning where is *my* car, given it was registered in *my* name." She looks at me. "Isn't that right, Kurt?"

I turn my eyes away.

"Oh, correction. I *was* the owner of a 1982 Skoda, until this morning."

Lincoln jumps to his feet. "You fucking what? You can't do that!"

"Oh yes I can. Ask Kurt, it's all legit. He was there, when the change ownership was signed in *my* name. That car was legally mine, but don't worry. I'll give you what I got for it." She pulls out a two-dollar coin and flicks it at him. He picks it up from the grass, staring fixedly at his fortune now shrunk to the value of a cheeseburger. The air reeks of lover's revenge and I'm bracing myself for what's next.

"Fuck! Fuck! Fuuuuuuck!" He clutches his head, begins to pace. "Why the fuck did you sell the car?"

She grins. "Let's just consider ourselves even. I'm out of here," she says. "So long."

"Wait! Who... what... where is it now, the car? Tell me it's still in town?"

Helen shrugs. "I sold it to this French guy. You should have seen the look on his face when I told him how much I wanted for it."

"Which French guy? Where's he now?"

She puts a finger to her chin. "Hmmm, let me think. The answer to your question... I don't know and... I don't care." She turns her back. Lincoln grabs her by the arm. "Let go of me!" she screams. I move forward, but stop as soon as he lets her go.

"Where was he heading? Give me something!" he pleads. "Please, you can tell me at least that."

She sighs. "For what it's worth, that car was a piece of crap. Why do you want it so bad anyway?"

"Just tell me!" he snaps.

"All right, all right. He said he was heading down the coast."

"East or west?"

"West, I think."

"What do you mean *you think*? They are completely different coasts. Which one was it?"

She frowns. "Well, he said he was heading to Greymouth or something."

"West. So he's heading down the west coast. When? Did he go this morning?"

She nods. "Yeah, I think so."

Lincoln turns away. "Shit, fuck!"

"Look, I've got to catch a bus." She pauses before walking off, looks over at me briefly and smiles. "Nice knowing you, Kurt."

"Yeah, you too, safe travels!"

There she goes, just as independent as when she walked into our lives. I'm pleased, for her sake, she's leaving. No doubt safer than sticking around with the likes of us. If anything had happened to her, I wouldn't have been able to live with myself.

Lincoln's pacing, pondering what to do next. He glances at me. "You know anyone heading down the west coast, like today, now?"

I look around, shake my head. I'm not sharing the level of distress he's in. Maybe because I'm just pleased to be back inside my head, back to normality.

He stops pacing, looks at me intensely. "You pack all our shit together and meet me out by the road, in say half an hour, okay?"

I shrug. "Why? Shouldn't we just stay here? It's safe, isn't it?"

"Look, I'm not going to argue with you, Kurt. Gather our shit and meet me out on the road. We're going after the Frenchy!"

"But… what are we going to do when…"

He runs over to the bike shed, picks out a spotty bike. "See you soon," he says, and starts madman peddling in the direction of town.

38

I'm not ready to leave. I don't want to leave. I've developed an affinity to this place, could easily hang here for the rest of the summer. However, while waiting for Lincoln, I've been thinking. The problem is not that our fortune has disappeared, but our salvation. The money is nothing more than a potential bargaining chip, a resource for our escape. Whichever way I look at it, without the money, we're sitting ducks.

I pay what I owe Sid, including Lincoln's share in camping fees. He asks where I'm heading. I tell him the west coast, maybe. Then I say I have no idea.

"Best way to go," he says, smiling. "But just remember what the dormouse said." He winks. "Safe travels, man."

I'm sitting on my backpack on the side of the road, waiting, when a car turns the corner at rocket speed. I'm assuming it can't be Lincoln, he would be slowing down by now, then the brakes slap on, the car angles straight for me. I leap into the ditch as a blur of vehicle skids past. There are about thirty metres of black tyre marks before he finally stops. Lincoln clicks open the passenger door, yells at me to hurry up. "Yeah, yeah," I say, climbing out of the ditch and brushing myself off. He reverses. "Get in the fucking car!"

I sling in our bags and get into the passenger seat of an old Mazda 323 – faded baby poo yellow colour. In the time it takes me to blurt out the words, "Where did you get this?" the car's already picking up speed, accelerating around a fifty-kilometre corner at eighty. What I notice is how pale he looks, and for the first time he's trembling, an actual tremor in his hands gripping the gear stick, chopping it back, wheels on the verge of losing traction. I tell him to slow down.

He eyes the rear-vision mirror and, surprisingly, steps off the gas, just enough to keep the thing on the road. "Hohepa," he says, glancing over at me. "I saw him, in town."

A wave of terror washes over me. "You fucking sure about that?"

"Yes, I'm fucking sure." He whacks the dashboard with his fist. "Damn it, how the fuck does he know we're here?"

The newspaper article is in the forefront of my mind, which I refrain from telling him about right now. "Did he see you?"

He nods. "Yeah, I think so. I mean, I'm pretty sure he saw me while I was hot wiring the car."

I sigh, shake my head. "Great. So, let's break this down. We're in a stolen vehicle being chased down by a psychopath while pursuing some French guy who has all our money." I stare at him. "Is that the same page you're on, because shit, Lincoln, our lives are really looking up right now."

He doesn't say anything, just nods, checks the rear-vision mirror. A lengthy silence ensues: the sound of the engine, the vibrating body of the car, the wind screaming past. My heart sinks as I farewell Golden Bay – it was good while it lasted. Back into the fire, back into the hunt and being hunted.

39

The tank is on empty when we stop in Motueka for petrol. Lincoln has to keep the engine idling, given it's hot wired, and if Hohepa shows we need to be ready to flee. I'm handling the pump, standing on the exposed side while Lincoln's crouching down out of sight.

Back on the road we take a right on a backcountry route towards Murchison. "Keep looking behind us," he says. "Any sign of a car following, tell me." I clamber to the rear, securing my role in the escape from a madman. Never mind that Lincoln is also mad and that I've found a copy of a *Lonely Planet* guide written in German. I'm envisioning some bewildered tourist right now, scratching his head in Takaka, groceries clutched in his hands.

Half an hour goes by, no sign of anyone tailing us. I return to the front seat. "I think we're in the clear."

Lincoln glances in the rear vision mirror, sighs. "We're not clear. Just because you can't see him doesn't mean shit. As long as we're in the same country as he is, he'll find us. We need to get off this island."

"You mean overseas? I thought you said airports were out."

"There are other ways of getting off this island other than through an airport." He looks at me, grins. "How are your sailing skills?"

Now I see where this is heading. "Great, another half-baked idea of yours. No way, man."

He laughs it off. Obviously I'm out of my head to even raise an objection. "You're not hearing me. Don't judge before you hear it."

Death. If Lincoln were to spontaneously die somehow that would solve the problem. No Lincoln. No connection to me, for eternity.

"My plan, and I've thought about this a lot, Kurt, is to buy a yacht. It doesn't have to be big, just as long as it's equipped with category one."

"Category what?"

"You know, so it can handle the open ocean. Has all the specs; VHF, inflatable lifeboat…"

I feel I'm already in a lifeboat.

"…beacons, flares, storm sails etcetera… I say we buy it in Fiordland, hug the coast, and if we're checked by the coastguard we'll just tell them we're heading to Stuart Island. Then we'll head out."

"To where exactly?"

He shrugs. "The Pacific somewhere. Ideally where authorities are slack with maritime law. I haven't thought that far yet. First, we need that money, unless you've got a spare fifty grand in your pocket for a boat." A long pause. "So, what do you think?"

I take my time before answering, gazing out the window at the long rolling fields of sunburnt grass – my thoughts singed to the point of exhaustion. I'd rather stop the car and thumb a lift with fate than entertain this warped desperate idea of his. Where to begin? I imagine myself on a yacht in the high seas with monster waves. All I can think of is that we're going to drown and the sense of drowning has already begun. Then I consider it being just Lincoln on his mad Captain Ahab mission out to sea – a much more palatable idea – a mild eureka even.

I turn to him. "Well, what I think is, I don't have to join you. I'll help you get the money, the boat and all that. I'll even wave goodbye from the pier. But going with you, that's not needed. Once you're out of the country my problem is over. Besides, I can't sail for shit."

Lincoln nods. "Yeah, okay. You sure though? It's the islands we're talking about here. Adventure, the unknown."

"Yeah, I'm one hundred percent certain. That adventure is all yours." I look across at him. "So, we've got a deal?"

"All right." He grips the steering wheel, his knuckles whitening. "Let's go get our money."

40

We don't stop in Murchison, and we don't blink either, keeping our eyes peeled through valleys of beech forest, following the Buller River as it snakes down to the plains and out to Greymouth.

"Where to now?" I ask, as we stop at a set of red lights.

Greymouth seems bigger when you're looking for something particular. We drive down the main drag, slowly. Every second shop seems to sell greenstone and bone carvings and other tourist paraphernalia. Tour buses line the street. Foreigners mill about with credit cards and cameras at the ready.

Lincoln drives up and down the main thoroughfare twice then off into various tributary streets, circling and weaving through town and the outer suburbs before finally coming to a halt. A red Skoda – easy to spot, but nowhere. "Maybe Helen was leading you down the garden path," I say.

Lincoln shakes his head. "Nah. All tourists come this way. Major tourist trap." He shrugs. "He could be anywhere around here. Gone for a bush walk, driven to Hokitika, West Port, Karamea?" He sighs. "I think we're going about it the wrong way. What we know is, once you've passed through Greymouth there is usually only one main tourist trail – down the west coast. We're better off hanging out in Franz. We could easily spot the Skoda passing through there."

"So, it's Franz Joseph then?"

He nods. "Yeah. Hohepa will be able to spot us a lot easier too."

I stare out the window. It begins to spit. Raindrops patter the roof. Then it seems like the whole Goddamn sky falls down.

On the next stretch of road all my problems seem dwarfed. To my left rise the Southern Alps – alpine giants towering over the west coast, and to the right crashing waves spitting ghosts of salty air. This is where nature gives the impression it's winning. The dusky caramel light coats over the snowy peaks and ridges of dark chocolate rock. They could be the ice cream treats for a bigger God about to dip down from the heavens with an enormous spoon.

I'm feeling momentarily contented, anesthetised by The Chills playing in the background and the soothing hum of the car.

41

We arrive after dark and check into a hostel. Expenditure is now covered by what's left of my drawn down student loan. I sign in our names as Hunter Thompson and Ralph Steadman. It's imperative we keep our identities hidden, especially now that we could be connected to a stolen vehicle, or if Hohepa shows we don't want to leave behind any crumbs.

Franz Joseph. A miniature model town. It would implode and vanish completely if it wasn't for the daily busloads of tourists all eager to get a close-up view of the glacier. Visitors from all over the world come to see this giant slab of slow-moving ice. Personally, I don't really see what the fuss is about, but am drawn to the air and the mountains.

Over a pizza and a couple of beers we decide we'll sit tight for a couple of days until Mr Frenchy shows up. It's unlikely he would have passed Franz yet, given the distance from Takaka. He may have gone a little further to Fox so we plan to scope it out first light.

We retire early into a dorm room filled with snoring tourists and rustling plastic bags. This doesn't bode well for a restful night. Maybe three to four hours of broken sleep is all we get before we're up slurping down a two-minute noodle breakfast.

As planned, it's Fox first thing, but when we wander out onto the street where the Mazda's parked, we freeze in our tracks.

Up ahead there's a guy bending over, his back to us, peering into our car. His face is hard up against the glass, his eyes shielded by his hands to block out reflection. His stocky build and long dreads give off a big enough clue who he might be. A loose turd is about to launch into my pants. Lincoln grabs me, pulls me inside. The sliding doors close automatically. "Fuck, Hohepa!" *Flight mode*. I'm running but the adrenaline has warped my world into a slow-moving nightmare. I'm right behind him and it seems forever to run the length of the corridor and into our room. "Pack all our shit, hurry!" I clump and push everything into my pack. This is not the time to itemise clothes, although it's tempting out of absolute denial this is happening. I'd rather pair socks and fold underwear in an air of fake calm than accept this reality.

Lincoln flings open the window, we jump out and move at pace over the back lawn, leaping a fence and another. We get out on the main road and slow to a normal but perilous stroll, eyes to the front, attempting to blend in as tourists. There's a line of coaches steadily loading punters. Lincoln spots an empty Kiwi Experience bus parked up with the door wide open and makes a beeline straight for it. He casually climbs on board and I follow him all the way to the rear of the bus. "Now, get the fuck down," he says.

We're crouched behind the seats, almost lying on the floor. Maybe ten minutes of silent terror pass. Then there are footsteps boarding the bus, and I'm relieved when I hear a thick rolling Irish accent and maybe a German or Swiss voice. As the bus starts to fill with friendly chatter and people finding their seats, Lincoln and I gradually sit up, trying to act inconspicuous. Lincoln whispers, "Let me do the talking."

The bus driver gets into his seat, followed by the tour guide who seems to almost bounce his way onboard – a hyper-energised gym bunny with peroxide hair – the over friendly type. Hopefully he is so far up his own arse he won't notice the likes of us. He slaps his hands together. "Okay, guys, next stop Queenstown. But before we go, *yo*, please look around to see if we're missing anybody." I can feel my face redden. I'm sure we're about to be sprung. Heads turn. A girl in front of us glances over her shoulder. I want to disappear. "Hey, where did you guys spring from?"

"My name's Hunter," says Lincoln. "And this is Ralph. We were on the previous bus, but missed it, if you know what I mean."

She nods understandingly. "Bummer, I know what that's like." She reaches over to shake hands. "My name's Kelly by the way." She could be American or Canadian. "Welcome aboard."

"Thanks," Lincoln replies, forcing his trademark grin. The girl smiles and faces the front. The engine starts. Lincoln taps me on the shoulder, points nervously. Outside, on the footpath, we can make out Hohepa striding towards the centre of town, his murderous wide shoulders, his monster-thick arms. We shrink ourselves below the window as the bus rolls by.

42

The gods have been good to us, especially now as we enter Queenstown with a clear evening sky and a wisp of cloud on the surrounding peaks. A gondola rises silently on the hill over streets filled with tourists and restaurants and bars and the never-ending vibe of Friday night. I swear Queenstown knows no other day.

We dump our gear in a dorm room shared with Americans, take a shower and head out to the bars. It feels therapeutic to pretend we're just on holiday and have nothing better to do than drink. What is blatantly obvious is the shift in the game. It's only about survival now. The chances of finding the Skoda are becoming increasingly remote. I'm sure Lincoln knows this but he refuses to spell it out. That would admit defeat which is not Lincoln's style. Instead, we are just drinking, numbing our minds, and it feels nice to drain beer outside the Dux Deluxe, enamoured by beautiful European women strolling by. It's an easy way to deny where my life is headed right now.

"Check her out," Lincoln says, audible enough for the girl to glance at him. "What a dream."

I take a long pull of my beer. "So, what's next?"

He doesn't even look at me, his eyes are firmly fixed on the next female walking past. "We're doing it, man. This is what we're doing. Drinking, okay. Tomorrow I'll think of something."

Hearing this I drain the glass. "Okay, drinking is what we'll do then." This is one thing that'll go according to plan, something that we are particularly good at.

43

I wake with a collection of sordid memories of last night: Lincoln flashing his credit card and purchasing a number of lethal cocktails over the bar, signing each credit card receipt with obscenities like *Fuck you*, *Balls*, *Arse tits* and other derogatory signatures the bartender never bothered to check. And myself, stumbling around on the dance floor until the lights came on and the music stopped and I recited Emily Dickinson poetry at the top of my lungs until I was ousted by some bouncer.

It takes a good part of the day to recover, sucking on water bottle teats and taking long morose walks along the lake edge. Despite the fresh mountain air and bluebird sky it takes forever for the hangover to lift.

When I return to the backpackers, Lincoln is sitting at a picnic table outside. He looks up as if he's been waiting for me. "Where have you been all day?"

I sit down opposite. "I've been retrieving my mind, and you?"

He pauses, looks at me with those intense blue eyes, and I can tell already he's got something important to say. "I've been thinking," he says. "About the money. I don't think we can waste time for Frenchy to show up. It's too risky just sitting here on the off chance. I'd say Hohepa will be here soon if he hasn't already arrived."

I tense up. "What, you think he's here?"

"I don't know." He shrugs. "Maybe. But the thing is I've got another proposal, to get the money that is." He writes something on a paper napkin and hands it to me. It reads: *Bank robbery.*

I shake my head. "You're fucking taking the piss, right?"

"Nah, I'm serious."

I laugh. "No way in a million years. No fucking way."

"But you don't even know what you're saying no to yet. Hear me out at least." He pauses, leans in. "You know as well as I do, we need this money, right?"

"To buy a yacht and for you to get as far away from me as possible. Yeah, I get that part."

"Yeah, that's it, but yachts don't grow on trees, do they?"

I nod. "So do it yourself then."

"What do you mean?"

I lean forward, lower my voice. "I'm not cut out for this shit, man. You have what it takes – class A scumbag. I'll only slow you down. You really don't need me on this."

He grins at me, takes my shit, almost gentlemanly. "Yeah, you're probably right there. I am a scumbag. Fair call. But you don't really have to do anything."

"Good," I interject. "Then I won't do anything. I'll just sit right here, leave it up to you."

"What I mean is, I just need you to do a couple of things."

I stand. "I'm out. This is absolutely crazy. What your idea needs is its own customised straitjacket. Forget it, Lincoln."

"But you haven't heard what I'm going to say."

"I don't want to hear it." I start to walk away.

He gets up, follows. "Where're you going?"

"Anywhere away from this conversation." He stops following and I stroll back into town, back to contemplating the clouds and mountains reflected in the lake.

44

No way. I'm not made for this, not strong enough, not mad enough to carry it out. I should leave, right now. Only, the sad desperate truth is, he's right. Sitting here is like waiting for a death sentence, and this option B before me now comes into focus, a little sharper.

I'm going to hear him out, at least listen to his plan. Does that make me an accomplice? I guess it does, although everything I've done up till now makes me an accomplice. So what's the difference? Nothing. I'm screwed either way.

When I return he's no longer at the picnic table, or anywhere else. His stuff has gone from the room. I ask the receptionist and she tells me he's checked out. I should be glad he's gone, relieved that's he's gone solo on the job. Most of me believes this, but a part tells me this isn't the last I'll see of him. It's too easy, him disappearing like that. What ought to be putting me at ease has done the opposite. What now? In which direction do I head? I realise this is the first time in the past few weeks I can ask this question independent of Lincoln and his plans. It scares me. I'm free, it seems, but free to do what exactly?

45

It's been two days. No Lincoln. No Hohepa. My existence
has never felt more temporary. I'm in limbo between two
worlds – a wafer thin space shrinking infinitesimally
smaller but never quite closing in. I don't quite know how
to behave. Do I relax, wait for something to show up, or
do I start running on the spot in a freak of panic? This is
fear without an object – what Kierkegaard called anxiety,
I think. Today is my birthday so I'm determined to sweep
this anxiety crap under the rug.

I start with brunch at a lakeside café. A stiff bloody
Mary with blueberry pancakes and the day seems a whole
lot more promising. Having rounded off the edges I sit
back and observe tourism go by. The click of cameras,
things to do, things to see. A group of Chinese tourists
stand at the lakeside edge taking photos of a pair of
waddling ducks. Despite the yawn and stereotype
prevailing this scene, how wonderfully simple and benign
this seems. I have overlooked the possibility that
contentment could be obtained without the rush of
adrenaline, or the idea I don't have to almost kill myself
for happiness. One thing's for certain, these tourists will
all probably sleep well tonight, including the ducks.

The waitress is coming over. I've been watching her ever since I sat down. There's a spring in her step, a contentedness as she glides from table to table, smiling at her customers, authentically, not the forced grin type. I'm envious of that smile, that lightness in her walk.

"Everything okay with your pancakes?"

"Everything's fine," I reply. "Although, I was wondering, do you have any Champagne?"

She hesitates before answering, probably registering that a customer is asking for more booze and it's not even midday. She smiles. "Sure."

"Do you have real Champagne, you know, the French stuff?"

"I think so, I'll check." She returns with the wine list. At the bottom they have a small selection. Champagne labels start from ninety dollars a bottle. What the hell am I doing? With the fortune gone I can't afford this. It forces an unwelcomed introspection. At twenty-two I've finished my degree and yet I don't fit anywhere. It's a terrible burden looking at my future from these trenches – no man's land. The only consolation is I'm looking at this waitress, at her eyes sparkling in my directionless haze. "Actually, come to think about it, I'll go with the cheaper option. The Lindauer, thanks. Just one glass."

"Sure thing," she says. "One glass of Lindauer."

Then seemingly from nowhere, I add, "Actually, make that two glasses, if you care to join me." It sounds cheesy, the words just slip out, but I'm beyond subtlety – the manifestation of a kind of bold confidence that wasn't in me before. *My God, maybe hanging around Lincoln is starting to rub off.*

She laughs nervously. "I'd love to, but you know, I'm kinda at work."

"Come on," I say. "Just a sip, a small toast. It's my birthday."

She smiles. "Really? Well then happy birthday. How old are you today?"

"Twenty-two," I say, then add, "It's a tough age, apparently."

"Oh yeah, how's that?"

"I heard it somewhere. Maybe over the radio. It made sense at the time." I pause, aware she's still standing there and could've easily found an excuse to leave. "How old are *you* by the way?"

"Me, um... I'm twenty."

I nod. "Good age."

"Oh, you think?" She blushes a little, tucks a loose strand of blonde hair behind her ear.

"Well, you're not expected to have a career at twenty. Rite of passage to be a student and go crazy kind of thing, until you hit twenty-two. Your degree is over, and if you're still studying it either means you've failed papers or you're studying something serious. The pressure is on. You have to finally make something of yourself. Yet I'm nowhere near a career. I have a degree and a lot of debt and a lot of questions." I pause, conscious that perhaps I've shared too much. She probably wasn't expecting that. *I* wasn't expecting that.

"Interesting perspective," she says, nodding. She looks around at the tables, pauses, then returns her eyes on me. "I'd better go, but it was nice talking. A glass of Lindauer, right?"

I'm getting a good vibe off her. She's probably just being friendly. I might have left my radar equipment on Mars, but it's worth a punt. And what's more I remember what Helen told me, that she liked it when I was bold enough to speak my mind. "Before you go, can I ask a favour?"

She stops, nods out of politeness.

"I'm, well, there's no one I know here. And it's my birthday, and I'm aware you might have a boyfriend so I can understand if you can't, but, I was wondering if you might want to join me for dinner tonight?"

She blushes, just a tad. I'm ready for her rejection and immediately regret my impulsivity.

"You're quite direct, aren't you?"

I clear my throat. "Well, actually, not usually."

"Tonight... um... yeah... okay."

I lean forward, a little startled. "What? You said yes?"

She shrugs. "Sure, why not? Where do you want to meet?"

"I have no idea. I expected you would say no."

She ponders. "Do you know the Loaded Hog?"

I flinch – not my kind of place. "Yeah. I think I know it."

"Well, next to it is a good seafood restaurant, Catch Twenty-two. That's if you like seafood."

"Sounds fine with me. What time?"

"Around eight?"

"Deal. Catch Twenty-two it is."

"Great, I'll see you then." She's about to turn away and I realise the awkwardness of the situation. She'll have to return with my order and pretend to be a waitress again, and I'll have to return to the role of the customer. Too weird, it could ruin everything. Why am I drinking in the middle of the day, anyway? "Um, hold on. Don't worry about the Lindauer. And, one other thing, I don't even know your name?"

She smiles. "Jasmine. But you can call me Jas if you like."

46

I don't quite know how it happened that I'm going on a date with someone who I thought would be totally out of my league. And maybe that is the correct stance to take. Probably nothing will come of it. Maybe she won't even turn up? Just thinking about her, though, gets me excited. *Too* excited. Better to think of something else, squash my expectations, otherwise I'll wind myself into a nervous mess and come across desperate.

I spend the rest of the morning walking around town, drifting in and out of shops, eventually stopping at a bookstore, picking up a copy of Kurt Vonnegut's *Slaughterhouse-Five*. I've been wanting to read this for some time but never getting my hands on it. I have it now, tucked under my arm and find a quiet shaded spot under a tree.

I'm still reading, on the final chapter, the final page, when Jasmine walks into the restaurant. In the book I'm about to find out who survives the fire-bombing of Dresden. I've been engrossed in this book all day and already rate it in my top five. It's that moment when you're conflicted between wanting to finish the book and realising that continuing to read will definitely kill all romance. Of course, I'm not that stupid. I put the book down.

She's wearing a light summer dress, red, flush with her healthy complexion. "What are you reading?" she asks.

I show her the cover.

Her eyes widen. "Great book."

"You've read it?"

"Hell yes. It's a classic. Where are you up to?" She sits down and it seems we've already cracked through the ice.

"Um, well." I pause. "I'm on the last page actually."

"Oh, I'm sorry."

"What for?

"For interrupting. You should just keep reading. I mean, when I'm on the last page of a book I hate having to stop. I know what it's like. Please, just finish the book. I don't mind, really."

I lift up the book. "You sure?"

"Absolutely." She smiles.

I start reading again. I'm distracted, unfocused, and look up briefly to catch her looking straight at me. She looks away, begins to twirl a finger around a lock of her hair. I return to the last page, but instead of seeing words I see the image of her, the warmth in her eyes, the perfect number of freckles on her nose and not a mention of make-up to manufacture her beauty. It takes a lot of focus to read, to slog through the words, which aren't actually sinking in but passing through as a collection of meaningless letters.

I have to re-read the same paragraph three times before I'm able to move onto the next paragraph, and at the same time I'm worried she'll think I'm retarded for reading so slow.

I finish, barely ingesting the page but get some closure on the book.

"So, what do you think of it?" she asks.

I put it down. "It... it was. Well, I loved it."

"Me too. Especially that stuff about the Tralfamadorians and their view of time."

I nod. "Only that we humans are stuck in time. But if we observed all of time – past, present and future in one hit – then we would realise no one really grows old and dies."

She smiles. "Or so it seems."

47

We've moved on to a bar. I can't recall much about the actual dinner, we gas-bagged so much. Jasmine talked about her studies at Otago, working towards a major in English with a minor in philosophy. I told her I did the same, but the other way around. She told me she's vegetarian but eats fish. She can't slaughter a cow, apparently, but argued there was nothing wrong with eating a porterhouse steak just as long as you can kill the cow it came from. I told her I couldn't kill a cow and often talked to cows, but I hadn't talked to a steak yet. It came off terribly, a lame joke, and yet she laughed, made me feel at ease.

We're seated in Utopia bar with our martinis. The music is soft lounge and there are low lying red lamps giving off a cosy atmosphere. I'm pretending to enjoy my martini, but after a couple of sips I give up. I say to her, "Don't know what James Bond was going on about. It's just ethanol with a strange aftertaste."

"Eating the olive helps."

"Helps what?"

"Helps with the aftertaste."

I eat the olive, take another sip. "Yeah, I think you're right." I swirl the remaining martini with the mixer.

"So, tell me. When are you leaving Queenstown?" she asks.

I stop stirring. "Why, you sick of me already?"

"No, of course not." She glances away briefly, trying to contain her smile, and returns with a more controlled affection. "I think you're interesting."

"In a weird way?"

"A good way. I just want to know how long you'll be sticking around."

I shrug. "I don't have any set plans."

"Really? You must have some idea where you're heading next?"

"Well, that's the problem. I have no idea. I'm in limbo, no real direction."

She sips her martini, places it down gently. "Funny. That's where I want to be."

"What do you mean?"

"Well, you know… travelling around and stuff, no set plans. You should be happy. You're free to do whatever you want."

"Freedom. You know what Jean-Paul Sartre said about freedom?"

She nods. "Yeah. We are condemned to be free. I took that paper too."

"That's exactly it, I feel condemned. The opposite of a holiday."

"Gee," she says. "Sounds heavy. Why don't you just decide on something and stick with it for a while. That might solve the problem."

"Yeah, maybe. I don't know what though."

"Well, I hope you stick around for the next couple of days at least. It'd be good to hang out." She blushes, looks away. A warmth fills the space between us. "Thanks," I say. "I mean, it's nice that you think that." I look away too, avoiding eye contact, because to look now might spoil everything. She might see something I don't want her to see. The air is thick with intimacy. Our eyes train back, staring into one another, just long enough to let each other know we've got something going on without saying a word.

48

She walks me back to the hostel. I stall when we get to the entrance, kind of stand there in a geeky vegetated state, unsure whether this is goodbye.

"Kurt, aren't you going to invite me in?"

"Oh. Sure, okay."

I open the door and lead her into the common room. It's quiet and empty. Not surprising given it's one in the morning. "You want a hot drink or something?" I offer.

"Sure," she says, and wanders around, looking at party photos pinned to the wall documenting the hordes of tourists who have passed through over the years. After staring at them for a while, she says, "They all look the same, don't you think?"

The jug clicks off. I pour two herbal teas and bring them over. "Yeah, I know what you mean. If you look at them long enough all the faces meld into one and you can almost imagine they are all thinking the same thought." I blow on the tea and take a sip.

"And what do you think that would be? Let me guess. Hey, look at me, guys, I'm in Queenstown, really really drunk!"

I nod, smile. "Exactly."

She sits down on the couch. I follow suit, leaving just enough space between us to indicate things could go either way, if she wanted it to. We sip our teas in silence. It was easier talking before, easier the whole evening until now, when someone has to make a move, or say something that might lead to a kiss. I don't want to do the stretch your arms out routine – too cliché. My tea is nearly finished. I put the mug down, walk over to the stereo and blindly pick out a half-scratched CD and slide it in.

"Ah," she says, "Good choice." Mazzy Star, *Fade into You*, begins to play. I sit back down, inwardly grimace as I lower my arm around her. She doesn't tense up, in fact she shuffles closer and lowers her head on my shoulder. The warmth of her head placed there and the eerie calm in the room and all compasses point magnetic north. It's my signal to face her. She closes her eyes. My lips are about to make contact when she smiles so wide I end up kissing her teeth. I withdraw a little.

She giggles, sweetly. "I'm sorry. You're welcome to try again."

We're alone in the dark, bar a small headlamp on the floor pointed at the ceiling for mood lighting. I'm relishing that of all the nights the dorm room could be empty, thank God it's tonight. My arms are firmly glued around her. She's grinding her hips into mine, communicating clearly that she wouldn't mind if I explore her body. How long have I been waiting for this? My virginity is finally given a chance to submit a full application. She's nibbling at my ear.

"Get your shirt off," she says. I can't remove it quickly enough as she yanks it off and pushes me down on the bed. Christ almighty, this is really happening, and fast. She flicks her long hair forward, kissing my chest in an imaginary line towards my belt buckle. Her hair is tickling my chest as she goes down, expertly loosening the belt. Within seconds my pants are stripped, but then tragedy strikes. The bane of my existence – my dreaded feet. Having anticipated this might happen, I had made a pre-emptive strike earlier, smothering them in gran's remedy. At least that would disguise the smell and she'd be none-the-wiser if the socks stayed on.

She yanks them off. A small plume of fine white powder disperses in the air. A momentary pause. We both look at what heinous crime has been unearthed. The effect of the powder is convincing – my toes could be a stunt double for a cadaver in a morgue. I wouldn't blame her if she got dressed and left, but she just looks at me and smiles.

"A wee problem with your feet?" She reaches down to her handbag and withdraws a condom, tears it open with her teeth, hands it to me.

While she removes her top, I'm trying to get the damn thing on. I thought this would be easy, but in the dark I'm definitely struggling. *Hold the tip*, I tell myself, *just like in those educational videos, and roll it down*. Only that it's not rolling down. Jas has stripped completely, now straddling my hips, waiting as I battle the latex.

"You've got it upside down,' she says.

"What, have I?"

She takes over. "Let me try."

With all the delay I've gone flaccid but as soon as she touches it, I'm rising to the occasion again and she gently rolls it on with ease. I don't say anything and just let her take the lead as she casts her hair over my face, gently kissing my forehead and down the ridge of my nose. She stalls, her hot sexed breath against mine, adjusting herself over my member. I should just let myself go, unfurl the sails. Thoughts start racing through my head as she has trouble getting it in. My God, not now, don't you even dare think of going soft. I tense up, thrust prematurely but entry denied. I try again, she grabs it, holds it steady but I can tell already it's on its way down. Damn it. Robbed. Damn my useless bastard prick for letting me down with this perfect goddess. She tries again, I grit my teeth, pray to the hard on god, the angels of stiff throbbing cock. I look down, it's bending, going soft, shrivels back like a turtle into its shell, the failure complete. I let out a disappointing sigh. "I'm, um… sorry. I don't know what's wrong with him down there."

She kisses me, tenderly. "Don't worry about it. You probably just drank too much." She lies down, lays her face and hand on my chest. "This is nice anyway." I'm running my fingers through her hair. "That feels nice too."

"Um… you probably should know something about me."

She looks up with a start. "I knew it. You have a girlfriend?"

I laugh. "No. It's not that. I'm, well, how do I put this? I haven't actually done *this* before."

She frowns. "A one night-stand?"

"No," I say. "And I do hope it will be more than one night. What I mean is, I've never actually done the wild thing before."

She grins, looks away so I can't see her smiling. "Oh, come on. You can't tell me this is your first time?"

I sigh. "Technically, given my performance a moment ago, I still haven't had a 'first time', unless you count that as actually having sex."

She looks up at me, crossing her hands, nestling her chin in my chest hair. "It doesn't matter, you know. I mean, I don't care if you're," she pauses, "inexperienced. In fact, I kinda like that. There's nothing worse than a guy who thinks he's Don Juan, then seconds later he's done. Those guys bore me." She moves up until her face is in line with mine. "I feel… comfortable with you, you know."

"That's good," is all I manage in my reply.

She buries her face in my neck, starts kissing across my face and ends with a passionate kiss on my lips. "You smell comfortable, too," she says.

I laugh. "So, I don't smell like bum. I'm pleased about that." I continue stroking her hair, travelling my other hand over her back until it finds its natural resting place on her butt.

"You seem to like my arse," she comments.

I close my eyes. "Yeah, I guess I do."

"Do you like anything else about me?"

"Let me think. Apart from your beautifully shaped butt, what else do I like about you?" I pause. "I can't actually think of anything."

She laughs, squeezes me. "Stop it. I'm being serious."

"Well, if you're that insistent, I guess I like your ears."

She looks up at me. "What do you mean?"

I search for the right words. "They're cute and receptive."

She smiles, rests her head back on my chest, breathes a sigh. "I like my ears too." There's a silence, then her hand starts gently tickling something down there. Whatever she is doing is heaven, but I don't want to say anything to jinx it. Let's just say, I'm rising to the occasion. There's no rubber this time. I'm mute, completely in her hands. She straddles me and my application is finally accepted.

49

"Hey, wake up. Kurt, wake the fuck up!"

Someone's pushing me – someone who sounds a lot like Lincoln. I haven't opened my eyes yet – resisting the reality that he has returned. At least she's still lying next to me, the only part in my life that is going right for a change and now Lincoln is here to destroy it.

He grabs me by the arm and starts yanking. "All right," I bark at him, and sit up. "What do ya want? Can't you see I'm with someone?"

"Get your clothes on. We need to go."

I stretch, rubbing my eyes. "Go where?"

"Look," he says, seeming stressed. "It's vital we go now. Ask questions later."

Jas sits up, covering her upper half with the sheet. "Who's this?"

I try to introduce her to Lincoln, but he snaps, "I haven't got time for this. You love birds say your farewells. We need to go!"

"Dude, why the rush?"

"One word," he says. "Hohepa. Comprehend?"

I nod, close my eyes. Decision is made – there's no way I'm going to get Jas involved. The further I'm away from her the safer she'll be. I look up at Lincoln. "Can I just have three minutes alone, man? Then I'll be with you, okay?"

"Sure. But make it one minute. I'll be waiting in the car."

He leaves. I look at Jas, her ruffed hair, her confused eyes. I place a hand on her shoulder. "I can't explain right now, but I have to go with him." I pause, realising how weird this sounds. "I really enjoyed last night, by the way. I want to see you again, after I've sorted some stuff out."

She frowns. "Are you skipping town, right now?"

I nod. "I'm sorry."

"How long for?"

I shrug. "I actually don't know at this stage, as weird as that sounds."

"Are you, like, in trouble?"

I lower my head. "How about I get your number or email or something." I reach down into my bag for a pen and the copy of *Slaughterhouse-Five*. "Here, write it in this."

"That's fitting," she says, scribbling in her details and handing it back. "I'm travelling back to Dunedin in a couple of days, you know. I need to find a flat before the semester starts." She looks away momentarily. "You should look me up, if you happen go by Dunedin on your travels."

"Happen?" I say. "I'm definitely going." I move in for a kiss, but she doesn't respond with the same enthusiasm. "I'll look you up, I promise."

She stares at the floor. "Yeah, I guess you will."

I lean forward, raise her chin to mine. "Hey, I really enjoyed hanging out with you, okay? In fact, I miss you already."

She returns a half smile.

I get out of bed, pull on my clothes and gather my shit. "I'll see you in Dunedin, okay?"

She nods.

I kiss her on the lips.

50

"Where did you get this rust heap?" I ask, sliding into an old Nissan Sunny, reeking of stale cigarettes. "Must be the fourth car we've acquired this trip. They seem to be getting worse."

Lincoln starts the engine and pulls away from the curb. "Yeah, but it's all I can afford at the moment."

"I'm shocked. What, you didn't steal it? Don't tell me you actually paid money for this?"

"Five hundy." He slows at a set of lights, looks nervously left and right. "Listen, man. We need to get out of Queenstown."

"Hohepa?"

He nods. "Spotted him this morning. He was trying to park up his Falcon along the lake front." He pauses. "Luckily he didn't see me."

"You sure about that?"

There's an awkward silence. The lights turn green, he cuts back the gears. "Hey, good news, I've worked it all out," he says, grinning. "I've been busy."

"Busy robbing banks, I'm guessing."

He laughs. "You know I can't do this alone, Kurt?"

"No. I don't know, Lincoln. I can't see why you can't do it yourself. You're pretty skilled at this criminal shit. I'm, well… a peace lovin' hippie compared to you. Hell, I'm even thinking of becoming a vegetarian."

Neither of us speaks again until we pass through Frankton.

"So," he asks. "Who was that hot bod I saw you with earlier? You've been bonking your little brains out while I've been doing all the work, huh. You should be thanking me."

"Her name is Jasmine, and she's not just a body. I actually like her."

"Well, isn't someone pussy-whipped?" He suddenly slows the car and turns left down a dirt road.

"Where are we going?"

He grinds back the gears, tyres skidding on the bends. "Training," he says. "Today we start our training."

"Whatever," I say, and stare out the window at the dry Otago landscape. The road winds down into a hidden valley and a small clearing on the bank of the Kawarau River. I think of Jasmine, a little piece of paradise stowed away, the warmth of her body next to mine, how incredibly nice that felt. Then this feeling gradually fades as the engine stops and the voluminous sound of white-water drags me back to this other world.

51

The plan, the training, the madness, all comes to a head when Lincoln reveals two double-barrelled shotguns. "Where the hell did you get those?"

He lays a shotgun on the hood. "Hold the barrel steady, will you." He pulls out a hacksaw and proceeds to saw through the black metal. The cut-off barrel falls into the long grass. "I stole them from a farm," he says, lining up the second one. "It was easy. The lock was a pissy little thing."

I nod. "You know how to use these... I mean, we're not actually going to use them, right?"

The second barrel falls by my feet. "Don't worry," he says. "It's all for the effect of terror. They're not actually going to be loaded."

Wow, I think maybe there is some humanity in Lincoln not yet explored. "So, I'm guessing you got two shotguns expecting I'm going to be holding one. Is that it?"

He looks up while filing down the ends of the barrels. "Jeez, Sherlock. You're really sharp today, huh."

I hesitate, swallowing hard. "I don't think I can hold a gun. Maybe I'd be better suited as the getaway driver."

He cracks up with laughter. "Yeah, that would be great, wouldn't it? Bunny hopping from the scene of the crime. My God, we wouldn't make a hundred yards before stalling." He shakes his head. "Getaway driver, good one, man." He picks up a shotgun and aims it at a Punga tree. He pulls the trigger. There's a sharp click in the air.

"So, what then do you want me to do, Lincoln, since I'm not going to be driving or holding a gun?"

He grins. "Here, have a feel of this." He hands it to me.

My arms drop a little with the unexpected weight. "It's heavy," I say.

"Good, you're now an accomplice. You've got your fingerprints all over that thing."

I instantly drop it into the grass.

"I'm fucking with you, Kurt. Pick it up, hold it like this." He picks up the other gun and demonstrates. "Make sure the butt of the gun is in the crook of your shoulder. Eye up your target along the barrel and squeeze. Simple."

"But why do I need to know this? We're not actually going to shoot anyone. They're not even going to be loaded."

"Just do it. I'll explain."

I hesitate, look around – not a soul in sight. I bend down to pick it up and position the gun accordingly.

"Don't just stand square on. No gunman stands like that. If you fired now, you'd just lose balance and fall back. Put one foot in front of the other, brace yourself. Show them you've fired a gun before, that you're not scared to use it." I reposition myself. "Now, point it at something."

"What, the Punga tree?"

"It really doesn't matter, anything."

I take this opportunity to point it straight at Lincoln.

"What the fuck, not me you idiot!"

"Sorry, it was just instinctual." I grin to myself and aim at the Punga. Squeeze. Click.

For the rest of the day, he's briefing me on the plan but I don't really give him my full attention. It feels like watching a film about some bank robbery and two minor characters, who will surely die off in the early scenes. Apparently, this is happening tomorrow, late morning. Lincoln reckons ten o'clock is ideal to storm the Westpac branch in Cromwell, given it's the quietest time for customer service. The fewer people in the bank the easier it will be to control, according to him. Cromwell is the ideal getaway town being on a major highway intersection. An escape in every direction, scenic routes, short cuts, back country roads. The role I'm supposedly employed to do involves training the gun over the customers, keeping everyone on the ground, terrorised, not letting anyone move. No one is allowed to leave, Lincoln tells me. Not even an old lady with a bladder problem, not even someone having a coronary.

"And you're expecting *me* to actually do this?"

Lincoln ignores my question and draws on a piece of paper the layout of the town. My memory of Cromwell is not the sharpest. Nothing stands out for me apart from the giant plastic fruit on a pole. It's the town mascot, this monument. If you don't remember anything else about Cromwell, you'll remember these two big arse peaches on a pole.

"The bank is located in an uncovered shopping arcade," he tells me, pointing to the map. "The advantage of its location are the immediate alleyways and closed views from the street. We can escape in any direction." He pauses, draws in a couple extra details. "Now, what I propose we do, Kurt, is when we leave the bank on foot, we make it seem we are fleeing west, when in actual fact as we turn the corner we go the opposite direction." He points to the map again. "Along this narrow alleyway here are no windows on the sides of the buildings – blank brick walls, with two large skips side by side. There's a nice little hiding place between these skips – not visible to anyone or any security cameras. It's unlikely anyone will be going down this alley, it's not a thoroughfare and businesses usually dump rubbish at the end of the day. This hiding spot is our safe zone, Kurt, where we'll be preparing our disguises, pulling out the guns, and where we'll return to disrobe. From here we'll just walk casually to the end of the alley where our car will be parked. Got it?"

I hate to admit it, but his attention to detail is kind of impressive. "Jeez, Lincoln. It's like you've done this before."

He nods. "It's all about the planning, my friend."

"So, what, you're saying you've robbed a bank before?"

He sighs. "Listen, man. I've done shit. Stuff you wouldn't have even dreamed of. But even if I had robbed a bank, I wouldn't be telling anyone about it, not even *you*. Rule number one with a bank robbery is, you do not talk to *anyone* about it afterwards. I mean, absolutely *no* one. This is a secret you take to the grave." He looks at me with his mad blue eyes. "You understand?"

I nod and look away, fearing that if I stare into them long enough my retinas will burn. "I understand. But what about fingerprints on the guns?"

"Rubber gloves," he says, pulling out two unopened packets of pink dishwashing gloves. "We'll wipe down the guns before use and won't open these until we steal the getaway car."

I nod. "Got it... Actually, I don't get it. We already have a car?"

He grins. "You don't know shit about robbing banks, do you?"

"Well, it's not like I majored in it."

"That car is in my name, Kurt. If someone connects us with the number plate – game over. If our fingerprints are connected with the getaway car – game over. You see what I'm getting at? No tracks leading back to us. No witnesses, no fingerprints, not a shred of evidence."

I nod. "Fully get it."

He sighs, looks over the plan he's drawn, flips it over and starts drawing on the other side. "There's a popular tourist spot on the Crown Range where they park and go for day walks. I've been scoping this place out and I've noticed there's always a handful of rental camper vans parked there. What better camouflage than to appear as a foreign tourist entering and exiting Cromwell?"

"Not a bad idea," I say.

"Trust me," he says. "It's a fucking great idea. We wait for a camper to roll up, watch them leave with their daypacks, and bingo. We've got plenty of time to hotwire the camper, and when the punters return to discover it's gone, they're going to report it stolen, right? It's a four-hour return hike. The job will have been done by then. But for argument's sake, let's say they only went halfway and came back in two hours or even earlier. Then, when they call it in, the first thing the cops will ask them is the registration and description of the vehicle, right? I bet tourists wouldn't have memorised the number plate. And the description – a Maui fucking camper. How common is that? The South Island is teeming with them." He pauses, for effect. "Kurt, bottom line is, we'll be arriving as unsuspecting tourists and leaving as unsuspecting tourists, but thousands of dollars richer. It's watertight."

Not wanting to seem sold on the idea I say, "Yeah, maybe, but what about the Nissan. Where are we going to park that without them noticing?"

"We're going to hide it, of course, a few metres down the road. We don't want to park it next to the van we steal, do we?"

I look out at the Kawerau River, a wide torrent of mineral blue flowing by. "Sounds like you've done your homework."

There's a long awkward pause, a moment filled with the sound of the river, cold and chilling.

"So, are you in or not, Kurt? I've got to know you're one hundred percent behind this, that you understand everything I've just told you."

I have butterflies in my stomach – blind, frantic, smashing into one another.

I nod. "Yeah. I guess I'm in."

52

I'm in a bad space. It's approaching dusk. I'm sitting alone on a boulder that's ten minutes-walk down stream, looking out at the turbulent rapids frothing white and violent. I have a grim feeling about all of this. The plan seems solid, but if the way I'm feeling now is the same tomorrow I'll just freeze and fuck it up. This is completely alien to me, alien to the core, but I have to accept there is no waking up from here.

The line I crossed at the outset seems a far distant border now. I'm kilometres deep in foreign territory about to cross yet another line, one I could never have imagined. Maybe this is the natural path of bad choices. The more you make the bigger the consequence. Or maybe this will all work out and the only thing required is a modicum of focus and commitment. This is not the familiar excitement of throwing myself into the unknown. This feels a lot different, like it demands something more of me. Perhaps my soul or whatever's left that is considered good and moral. What is at the heart, the absolute core of my being, is that I cannot do this. The guilt and whatever comes from crossing this line with all the checks and balances, is not worth it. I need to tell Lincoln. But the moment I open my mouth he'll concentrate his power to convince me otherwise. I cannot allow this, which means the only option is to disappear, desert him right now. I've got all I need – my wallet and the clothes on my back. I look behind at the Nevis Bluff – a sheer fifty metre cliff straight up – the perfect way to slip past him. If he comes looking for me, he might think I've fallen into the river. I follow my eyes along graded ledges connecting and leading all the way to the top. I could climb that. No ropes. There's still enough light. I could reach the road and hitch an escape from here.

Exposed, alone. Thirty metres up and death is only a misplaced foot away. A heightened sense of nerves. There is nothing else I'm more focused on, grounded in, than this moment right, here. Tension. My buttocks are tensed. My eyebrows and jaw are tensed. Only the present matters. The past and future disappear.

I'm doing okay. Except my palms are sweating and I'm getting the dreaded shakes. At forty metres my legs are trembling up and down like the needles of a sewing machine. My peripheral vision blurs – I'm getting the fear, trying to hold back the flood gates of adrenaline. I look around for the next holds, realising that the face I *was* climbing on is now just loose interconnected slabs. I gently place my foot onto what I think is secure – a shelf of rock slides away. *Shit!*! My mouth dries up – the flood gates release. Handholds turn into compacted mud. I have no choice but to grapple with sinewy weeds sprouting from the dirt. This isn't rock climbing, it's mud wrestling, and the weeds are starting to pull from the roots. I'm bashing my Teva sandals into the dirt, trying to find purchase. *Why the fuck am I climbing in sandals? What the fuck am I doing here? You idiot!*

The full gamut of my stupidity narrows to one frightening realisation – not only am I high enough that if I should fall, I will force my head down through my arse on impact, there is also a grade six river waiting below – a series of lethal hydraulics that'll swallow me into a watery grave. I'm getting death-chills. My feet are pedalling in the loose mud. I reach for more weeds, the left weed rips, but the right holds. My feet stop sliding, and just for a second I'm frozen. My nuts drop. One metre above is the road with the metal barrier bending around. If I could just reach for that barrier, I would be safe, but getting there is another matter. There are two options on the table: grab another weed, knowing if that rips I'm surely doomed, or take a gigantic leap.

I begin to slip...

53

I don't know how Lincoln has slept so well. He actually rubs sleep out of his eyes when he wakes beside me in the tent.

"Slept well?" I ask.

He yawns, stretches. "Yeah, like a baby."

"Great to hear. I didn't get a wink."

He checks his watch, completely ignoring what I said. "Operation Cromwell has begun. We need to be on the road in like fifteen minutes."

I laugh. "Why does it have to be called that?"

He shrugs. "What's wrong with Operation Cromwell?"

"Sounds lame. Why not Operation Bank Heist, or Operation Get Your Arse Shot Off by the Armed Defenders Squad?"

"Shut up while you're still ahead, Kurt."

We roll up the tent and stuff down a breakfast of bananas and dry bread. Lincoln's wearing a look of intensity and focus, and when everything's packed, he orders me to get in. I stall for time, take one last look at the river. I just want to stay here where it's safe and peaceful.

"Get in the car!"

"All right, keep your hair on."

Ten minutes of driving and I have a bad case of nerves. My hands are shaking. With no sleep, I'm feeling a little disembodied. Lincoln notices. "Man, you look like shit. Just relax. All you need to do is follow the plan, as I told you."

"I think I'm... well..."

"Shit," he says, and pulls over, cuts the engine. "I'm not doing this alone, Kurt. Are you in or not? I need to know."

I open the car door and vomit onto the road. I sit back in the seat, wipe my mouth. "I guess I'm not used to this." I look at him directly, the longest I've dared to stare into those eyes. "Let's go," I say. "I'm committed. I swear on Sartre's grave."

"All right," he says, grinning. "Sorry for doubting you." He pulls out onto the road.

54

So far everything is going to plan, except Lincoln hotwired a Kea Camper instead of a Maui. I'm sitting in the passenger seat wearing pink dishwasher gloves – Lincoln insisted. No fingerprints on anything, here on in. It makes it difficult to open these CDs I found in the glove box, mainly German bands, except for Salmonella Dub. "Well, at least these tourists have good taste," I say, sliding it into the player. I turn it up real loud, try to drown out my inner voice telling me what I'm about to do rubs every ethical bone in my body the wrong way. However, it is not stupid. It is not insane or irrational. It is necessary and vital not to fuck this up, because getting caught will mean a definite squeeze on my liberties. Freedom – it's true, I possess it now. I'm not making a bad choice. How I see it, I already made that choice back in Wellington and now I'm just riding it out to its conclusion. I'm petrified, hiding behind a facial expression that doesn't quite fit. I want a happy ending. I'm trying to picture myself at the end when it's all over. But the nausea, it resurfaces again. For no reason other than to distract myself I rummage through the glove box and find a small bottle of pills. The label reads: *Diazepam*. "Hey, check this out?"

Lincoln looks at it. "Valium."

"This is Valium?"

"Yeah, and I think you should take one. It will calm you the fuck down."

I pop one onto my rubber glove. It's small, innocent looking. Lincoln glances at it. "Actually, that's a ten mg. I would just take half."

"All right," I say, breaking it in half. I swallow one half, and when he's not looking, I swallow the other just to make sure it calms me the fuck down.

The sky is airbrushed blue from up here. As we come over the Crown Range making our descent, I finally build up the courage to ask. "How much do you think we'll get?"

Lincoln turns down the volume. "Huh?"

"How much money you think we'll heist from the bank?"

He shrugs. "I don't really know. Enough, I hope?"

"What's enough? I mean, if our take is a just a couple of grand, I can't see how this could be worth it. I thought banks were prepared for guys like us and just keep a small amount of cash in the tills." I pause. "Tell me this whole thing isn't just riding on the tills?"

He changes down the gears as we approach a bend. "Well, aren't you the expert all of a sudden." He goes quiet, like he's trying to figure something out.

"Well. Is that what we're going for?"

He looks at me, agitated. "Of course we're not just doing the tills. The main supply is kept out back."

"Out back where? In a safe?"

"Yeah. In the fucking safe. Where else?"

I nod. "Good, I was just wondering, that's all."

"Just stick to what I told you. Your job is to cover me, keep the public on the floor. Let me do the rest, got that?"

"Yes, boss. Got it."

55

The camper is parked. Into the alleyway we stride, purposefully. I'm definitely feeling less stressed, in fact a little too relaxed for what is about to happen. Lincoln's carrying a large duffle bag, and when we duck out of sight between the two skips, he unzips it and removes the guns, beige bath robes and two rubber masks.

"Cool," I say, picking up my mask. "I've always wanted to be a clown." They look like something out of Stephen King. Bright orange hair, ghoulish grin. I don't ask about the extra-large bathrobes as we slip them on, assuming they are all part of this excellent disguise. I'm staring out of two rubber eyeholes. The intense rubber smell takes me back to when I was a kid, pulling costumes from a chest.

"Kurt," he says, grabbing me.

"What?"

"What are you doing? It's no time to sit down."

"I just want a little rest before we do this. Just a wee kip to re-energise."

"No you don't," he says. "Get the fuck up."

"It's the Valium," I complain. "I'm feeling tired." I stand, bracing myself against the skip.

"You ready?"

I nod, although realise he can't see my grin. "I feel like a clown."

"We're not just any old clowns, man. We're badass clowns. We're their worst kind of nightmare. Got it?"

I nod. "Badass. Got it."

We slip out from the skips and creep along the side of the alley. Lincoln pokes his head around the corner, views the entrance to the bank, pulls back to the wall. "It looks okay," he whispers. He cocks his gun and slides in two shot gun cartridges.

"Hey, I thought we weren't loading them?"

He locks his gun in place, pauses and looks at me – his eyes are like intense blue flames smouldering out of his mask. I can't help being amused at how freaky he looks, how all this seems to be some bad movie starring two orange haired idiots. "Listen, Kurt. Your gun is already loaded, okay. So be fucking careful."

I step back, holding out the gun. "Really, this is loaded?" I say aloud.

"Shush! Keep your fucking voice down."

I lower my voice. "Why are they loaded?"

"Relax," he says. "We're not going to shoot anyone. It's psychological. If they were empty, we'd behave like they're empty. Comprehend?"

"Okay dokey. It's your show, man."

"On the count of three then, ready?"

I nod.

"One."

As he begins to count, I try to imagine myself holding this gun, hiding behind this mask, threatening innocent lives.

"Two."

This is it. I lean against the wall, close my eyes, steady my breathing.

56

Yesterday at the river...

I begin to slip... but then hold it somehow, teetering, about to plunge fifty metres onto rocks. Out of nowhere, a pair of jumper leads drop down in front of my face, just dangle there, teasingly. Thank God! My singular focus is to grasp this lifeline.

I grab hold and go hand over hand, gaining grip of the road barrier. I'm safe, *I've made it.* I look up to acknowledge the rescuer. My heart starts beating like a death metal drummer. I almost let go. In fact, letting go might be the better option. I shuffle left. He moves left. I shuffle right. He moves right. Nope, he's not an illusion. I was hoping he was. I've been hoping about a lot of things lately, especially getting out of this alive. But I can't see an escape. I glance over my shoulder. If I leap out really hard, like a bat, there's a chance I might make the river.

"I wouldn't try it if I was you."

I stop shuffling, realising that if I'm not going to jump the very least I could do is play it innocent. "What's this about?"

Hohepa chuckles – one of those dry mean laughs. "Oh, I think you know what this is about." He removes his shades. I was expecting his eyes to be that of a pit-bull terrier, but they seem more intelligent than that. "Let's cut the bullshit act, shall we? I know that you know, Kurt. In fact, I probably know more about you than you know about your pal Lincoln."

His voice, how he talks is more articulate than I expected. I'm trying to keep my guard up, but it's hard when the monster you imagined has just rescued your sorry arse. "How do you know my name?"

"Seems like you made a lot of friends in… what do they call that camp?"

"Hangdog."

He smiles. "Yeah, that's it. Hangdog."

I brave a look at him. "The photo. It was the photo in the newspaper, wasn't it?"

He nods. "Good. Now you're getting it."

I spit out the words like I've been poisoned. "What…-what are you going to do to me?"

His grin contorts his face, wrinkling the rings of Saturn on his forehead. "You think I'm going to ask you a few questions, then dispose of your body, huh?"

I look down, try to find solace in the small bits of gravel on the road.

"What has Lincoln been telling you? Oh, I know. He's been saying I'm some kind of psycho, right?"

I nod, unsure as to why.

He folds his arms. "So, you agree I'm a psycho?"

I shake my head.

He laughs confidently. "I don't think you know what I am. But be sure of this, if I wanted you dead you wouldn't be standing in front of me right now. I think you owe me, at the very least, a moment of your precious time." He points casually with one finger towards his Falcon parked against the shoulder. "Ten minutes, that's all I ask."

I glance at the Falcon. There's another car parked in front a little further down the road – it's occupied by some dark figure – some accomplice keeping watch. I could do a runner, but where would I run to? By the time I make a few yards I would be mowed down. Besides, Hohepa knows who I am, and who knows what else he knows. He's probably already got the details of my family, where they live. There is nowhere to hide. I climb hesitantly over the barrier. Hohepa grins as he has me lead the way. I sense our shadows converge. I'm trying to convince myself that all he wants to do is talk. There is no real fear to be had. Everything will be fine. It's my trembling hands that betray me.

Hohepa gets the door. "Step in," he says. I get in and the door closes with a definitive click.

The interior has all the usual paraphernalia: fluffy dice, miniature skull on a chain, stale cigarette butts sprouting from the ashtray. So far I'm not completely out of my comfort zone, until Hohepa gets in the back and sits directly behind me. I try to turn around.

"Don't fucking look at me."

I return my gaze to the dashboard. The heat and fear have arrived in a massive wave. I regret not jumping now. Maybe I could still try? I sneak a glance at the door.

"Don't even think about it, maggot!"

My eyes return to the front. This is it. All the doom I've been waiting for. I can hear his leather jacket creaking menacingly as he prepares something. He leans forward, grabs my arms and bends them behind the seat, lashing each wrist with what is likely the jumper leads that a moment ago saved me. My arms are restrained. There are no second chances, my nine lives spent. I'd rather be that unidentifiable body mashed on the rocks than endure what's about to happen next.

A long silence. He's not saying anything. So, I figure I should just tell him everything since I have nothing to lose. I barely open my mouth and get a syllable out, when he cuts me off. "Shut the fuck up!" I hear him tearing off something that is likely... yep... I guessed right – a big wad of duct tape right across the mouth. I have a sneaking suspicion I've been in this position before. I suppose I ought to start begging for mercy, mumbling under the gag and sweating tears. But I know it's just a waste of time. Christ, I'm starting to feel like a seasoned expert at this, except this time I'm not harbouring the same hate. Hell, I can almost see the fairness of the situation. To him we stole all his money and killed his pal. The fact I'm still alive is a miracle. But the person I really blame, apart from Lincoln, is my own stupid self.

"You know, Kurt, have you ever thought about the shape of your skull?"

I nod. I'm just a puppet now, no strings attached.

"It's kind of narrow at the front and back. I bet your mother gave birth to you easy. You would've gushed out."

I nod again, and then think better of it. I shake my head, hoping he'll let me talk. But it doesn't seem to change shit. He leans in close. I can smell his ugly breath on the side of my face. "Your death can be easy too, Kurt."

My breathing labours heavy through my nostrils. What? Is he serious? It's not whether I comply and get out of this alive, he's giving me two ways to die – the hard way or the easy way. *Fucking Christ! Jesus! I can't breathe! Death. This is fucking it!* My nostrils are flaring, I'm hyperventilating, feeling lightheaded, about to faint when he rips the duct tape clean off. I take in an enormous gasp of air and straighten. My eyes focus on a familiar object he's got dangling in front of me. It's the same eleven inches I recall Lincoln shoving down Kane Mason's throat.

"Suck on this," he says, pushing it hard into my mouth, but I resist, pursing my lips. He pinches my nose. I'm holding my breath as long as I can. "Come on, open up, you know you want it." I can't hold off any longer. My mouth opens and in slides this huge rubber cock. He rams it to the back of my throat. I'm gagging, so he pulls it out and begins to slap my face with it – wet rubbery slaps. "You dirty fucking maggot!" He rams it in again, a horrible gurgling, tears streaming. My mouth just a raw hole for his hate.

Then he stops, removes it. I go all slack jawed. My face relaxes. His voice comes in, crystal clear. "If you want to live then you must tell me everything."

I nod.

"I can't hear you!"

"Yes! I'll tell you everything. Whatever you want!"

"Good," he says. There's a pause and I hear him adjust himself on the backseat. "Where's the money?"

I lower my head, grit my teeth. "We don't... well, you see..."

"Spit it out!"

"We don't have it!"

"Then where the fuck is it?"

I take a deep breath and tell him the whole story, how Kane died, Goddamn everything. He lets me talk uninterrupted. It's a stream of stale piss that's been brewing in me way too long, and it's gushing out like a Goddamn confessional, even our plans for the bank robbery.

"Sorry," I say at the end, lowering my head. "I'm... I'm truly sorry."

He sighs, clears his throat. "I guess that might explain the guns I saw you guys with earlier today, huh. Tell me, what about the safe? You do know there's fuck all to be had from the tills."

"Uh... he didn't mention a safe, come to think of it."

He claps his hands together, leans close to my ear. "Listen, and listen good! If I had got to you before the findings of the pathologist's report was known to me, then you'd have been axed into tiny bits, buried already, got it?" He pauses, leans back. "Those fucking lollipops. He was always sucking on those fucking lollipops. I always said that shit would kill him." He leans in again. "I don't know how the fuck you escaped and how fucking careless you have been with the money. But know this, if you don't do exactly as I tell you then you know what will happen?"

I nod with a certain ferocity.

"Excellent. Listen fucking good then. Do exactly what I'm about to tell you. Got it?"

I swallow. "Absolutely."

"Because you know what will happen if you don't?"

"I will die a horrible death?"

"Fucking right you will. But if you pull it off you might get your little pathetic life back."

I clear the massive lump from my throat. "What about Lincoln? What will happen to him?"

"Don't you worry about Lincoln. You just worry about yourself. You fucking clear on that?"

I nod. "Crystal."

57

"Three!"

I open my eyes. They have never been more open than they are now. I'm behind him, running, hot on his tail, gun gripped. We descend on the Westpac entrance. There's no one around. Oddly quiet. Lincoln almost face-plants into the glass doors. Christ! Perhaps they had seen us on camera and have gone into emergency lockdown? Lincoln purposely stands under the sensors, waves his arms. The doors stay closed. It's dark inside. No movement. "Shit," I say. "They knew we were coming. We're fucked!" I'm ready to run, bolt.

"Hang on," he says.

"What the fuck are you doing?"

Lincoln goes right up to the glass, peers in. "There's no one in there. Not even a single light on!"

"Let's get the hell out of here. It's a trap!"

He steps back. Then we both see it at the same stupefied, dumbstruck moment. A public notice stuck to the inside of the glass: 'CLOSED on Anniversary Day'.

"You fucking retard!" I say.

He turns to me, shrugs. "How the fuck could I have known that?"

"You could've checked a calendar, fool."

"Don't call me fool. *Fool!*"

We stand there, paralysed by the non-event, stewing in our retarded-ness.

"All right, whatever."

We run back around the corner, hide between the skips, remove the bathrobes, masks, stuff it all in the bag. Muppets – that's all we've amounted to. A pair of numb-nut muppets. Dejected by our spectacular failure we get back into the camper. Lincoln re-hotwires the engine, puts it in gear and we roll out empty-handed. "Fuck," he says, bashing his hand on the wheel. "Fuck, fuck, shit bag, enormous arse *cunt!*"

"Hey. Watch your language!" comes a voice from the rear.

I'm unsurprised. Two barrels of steel poke forward and rest at the back of Lincoln's neck. He jolts, almost swerves off the road. "Just drive," Hohepa barks. "Don't even think of turning around."

58

It's been half an hour since we left Cromwell. My left wrist is cuffed to the door with an industrial strength plastic tie, tightened with a one-way cleat. Lincoln's left hand is cuffed to the steering wheel. Hohepa hasn't allowed us to speak. Each time Lincoln tries to say something he gets two barrels pressed against his skull. I'm hoping he'll let me go soon, given my nagging concern. Hohepa hasn't looked inside the bag. I've got this sick feeling our deal will turn sour when he looks inside that bag.

"Um... Hohepa?"

"What?"

"I was wondering when you were going to let me out. Anywhere is fine, really."

He grunts. "Okay, all right, fuck it."

Lincoln's looking at me in disbelief. Everything has twigged and now I'm not sure who's my biggest threat. "Kurt, you fucking traitor!"

Hohepa slaps him on the head, twice. "Fuck up!"

Lincoln's ordered to stop by the side of the road. My mind is a lethal cocktail of fear. Any second now and I'll be free from this nightmare. He's about to hand me a pocketknife, cut me loose, when he stalls. "Hang on," he says. I hear the zip opening. I close my eyes.

"What the… Where's the cash?"

"Still inside the bank," Lincoln says.

"What the fuck do you mean?"

"The bank was closed."

"How can the bank be closed on a Monday?" Hohepa points the gun hard up against his head. "You fucking with me, yeah?"

Lincoln winces, "No, we're not fucking with you. It's a public holiday."

He turns to me, "Is he lying, Kurt? Tell me he's fucking lying?"

I shake my head nervously. "Nope. Unfortunately, he's not."

He lowers the gun, retreats to the back. "*Fuck*!" He punches the wall. We avert our eyes. The van reverberates with his punching and kicking. Then he stops and all we hear is the anger in his breathing. He slowly moves to the front.

"So, can I go now?" I ask in a pleading voice.

"No way, maggot. Drive!"

59

Death. The idea consumes me. The hollow emptiness beyond. Even worse if it were slow and painful. It will probably be quick. I hope for a quick end, marched out into some remote bush, ordered to kneel, buried in a lush valley set back from the Milford Sound, which I'm pretty sure is where we're heading. We've passed Te Anau and from here there's just one way in, one way out. The foothills of the Darren Mountains loom above. Dark clouds roll in out of meteorological necessity, although one could easily assume for theatrical effect. Yet, I convince myself it could be worse. Having to explain to my parents why I've taken this moral deviation, could be worse. Being buried in some Auckland cemetery, where all the dead North Shore people go, could be worse. At least I'll meet my end in nature, be it against my will.

I keep up this self-talk while the other part of me is locked inside my brain, naked, screaming. But there's no point venting that. It would only make things worse. Keep things philosophical. Imagine some eastern transcendental passing into the spirit world – those ridiculous pictures new age artists draw – *yes*, that's where I'm going, into the soft pastel colours where unicorns and dolphins frolic in higher dimensions. Breathe in, breathe out. Relax. It's a journey, and this part of your journey ends, ignore that part of yourself that is screaming – *What a load of horse shit! You're going to die!*

Breathe in, breathe out. Pastel colours.

Deeper into the valley we go. Mist and wet granite cliffs tower above. Lincoln's driving slower now, stalling for time, when suddenly a lone dog stands directly in our path.

"What the hell?" Lincoln hits the brakes, tyres screech to a stop.

We can't believe what we're seeing – a wet friendly pooch, a seeming apparition out of nowhere. This stray golden Labrador sits on its haunches, wags his tail, shows no sign of moving.

"Toot the horn," Hohepa instructs.

Lincoln gives two short blasts, but the Lab doesn't seem bothered at all, just sits there wagging his tail then moves towards us, limping, sniffing the front bumper. Lincoln begins rolling forward, slowly. Two barrels nudge at his head. "Hey, did I tell you to drive?" The van stops. Lincoln shakes his head. "I thought—"

"You thought, what? Perhaps you should've thought harder when you decided to steal from us, fuck head. Don't think. I do the thinking from now on, got that?"

Lincoln nods. "Got it."

"Beep the horn again."

Two more blasts.

"Again!"

Several blasts, but the dog doesn't budge. Then we see it. Two black tyre marks heading off the edge of the road. Hohepa sighs, "Ah shit... pull over, kill the engine!"

Lincoln reaches down with his free hand awkwardly to disconnect the wires. The engine cuts out, and now we can hear the pattering rain and a distant sound of a river, and if we strain our ears an unmistakable moan. "We should check it out," I say.

"You maggots are going nowhere." Hohepa gets out and walks around to the driver's side, opens the door. "Just in case you get any fancy ideas," he says. Lincoln obliges, lifting his other arm, so now both of his hands are tied to the steering wheel. No way he could reach the wires if he tried. He waves the gun at us. "No funny business, got that?"

Lincoln and I nod in unison. He conceals the sawn-off in his jacket and starts down the bank. We watch as he disappears from sight.

"So, he's not a psychopath after all," I say.

He looks at me. "What do you mean?"

I shrug. "I'm just saying maybe he's not as cold and callous as you might think."

"What? You think he's not going to go through with it? Get real, Kurt. If we don't find a way out of this, we're fucked, got that? Why do you think he's taking us all the way out here? He's finding us a nice little burial site."

"So what now?"

His eyes widen. "You're asking me? Like I've got to bail us out all of sudden. If you hadn't gone behind my back then we might've had a better chance. What the hell were you thinking?"

I shrug. "I just thought, if we actually heisted the money, we could have paid our way out. Pity you picked a public holiday."

"So now it's my fault, huh?" He looks away, agitated, tries to jiggle his hands free. "Ah... forget it. All that matters now is finding a way out of this. You've got a hand free. Try to find something sharp to cut us loose." I open the glove box and search through, nothing but tissues and lolly wrappers and empty CD cases. I bend down, search blindly under the seat, get a grip of something metal, lift it up.

An ice-scraper.

"That'll do," says Lincoln. "Hurry!"

The edge is blunted, but with a repeated stabbing motion I soon make inroads on the plastic tie, creating little indentations. I try yanking my wrist away from the handle, hoping it will break, but instead the whole handle comes off.

"Great," Lincoln says. "Now me." I shuffle over, about to start bashing away. "Hold it," he says. "It'll take too long. There's got to be something sharper." I clamber over the back, look around wildly, pull open the kitchen draw. Bingo! I climb into the front seat gripping a Swiss Army pocketknife. I start sawing into the left plastic tie when I see Hohepa, his back turned, dragging someone up the bank.

"Too late," Lincoln says. As Hohepa makes the road he turns around just in time for me to plant my arse on the seat and loosely position the handle back to how it was. The cut to the left tie hadn't gone far enough, but if Lincoln pulled hard he could break free, which at this moment he doesn't even dare. Hohepa eyes us for a second and returns his attention to the crash victim. There's blood running down the guy's face, eyes bruised shut, he's unconscious but he's still got colour. Hohepa drags him a little further and lays him on his side. The dog comes over wagging his tail, sniffing his owner, licking his face.

"Be ready," Lincoln says, muttering under his breath.

"Ready for what?"

"Let's just say we might have us a little crash of our own."

I'm about to protest when Hohepa turns towards us. "Just be ready," Lincoln whispers under his breath. "And don't lose the knife."

Hohepa gets back in the camper, reaches over and cuts the right tie releasing one of Lincoln's hands. "All right, start her up," he says.

"You're just going to leave him there?" I ask.

"He'll live. Someone will see him and pick him up. Let's go!"

60

I'm second guessing everything. A cold-blooded killer doesn't stop to help a crash victim. It just doesn't compute. Yet Lincoln's certain there can be no other fate than our sorry arses buried six feet under.

I have the knife wedged in my pocket, ready. What's Lincoln got planned? Drive off a cliff kamikaze style? Ram us into a tree? I have no idea, but I prepare myself for something nasty, brutish and short. There can be no pleasant ending, I'm resigned to that fact. Hold on, hold onto what – hope?

An hour goes by which feels equivalent to a week sitting on death row. Hohepa orders him to take the next right, just after the bend. Lincoln nods, chops back the gears to make a sharp turn down an unmarked metal road. The thick canopy of vegetation overhead engulfs us as the road narrows, barely wide enough for the camper. Fist-sized stones and ruts strike the camper's undercarriage. "Keep going, all the way to the end." We continue for a kilometre of the same, until there's light at the end of the road. The sound of the voluminous Hollyford River can be heard over the engine. I can see the rapids now, spitting aggressively white between the clear breaks in the trees.

Lincoln glances at me. "Grade four, perhaps grade five white water. What do you reckon, Kurt?"

"Hey, shut it," says Hohepa

What the hell is he talking about river grades for? Then the penny drops… ah, shit. I think I know what he's about to do. My body freezes, except for my hand that somehow manages to stealthily unwind the window, an inch. That should better my chances, perhaps.

Two hundred metres and closing. I can see Hohepa's blue Falcon parked up ahead. He must have had help getting it there, then I recall he had an acquaintance with him when he interrogated me back at Nevis Bluff.

Lincoln's not slowing down.

One hundred metres. To my left is a clear drop down to the river, flowing parallel to the road.

"All right, you can slow down now," says Hohepa.

Twenty metres.

"*Hey*, slow the fuck down!"

Lincoln plants the throttle, yanks the steering hard left.

Wheels leave the ground. Silence.

Ladies and gentlemen, fasten your seat belts. Expect turbulence.

61

White and violent all around me, held down by the hydraulic claws of the river, waiting to be flushed.

The surface is somewhere up there.

Just relax, I tell myself, don't fight, be still in this cold watery grave and soon you'll be let out. But this doesn't stop the stages of grief running through me in one tightly pinched breath. Denial. Anger. Acceptance. I'm going to die. Air. I need to breathe. I need to breathe *now*. This is it. My chest tightens. Flecks, spots, everything darkens. Then I break through, inhaling life back into my lungs.

Swim. *Swim!*

I throw my arms in front of me. My technique is like someone in the grip of an epileptic seizure. I'm making headway, swimming diagonally cross-current. The water is colder than a witch's tit, and it's turning my limbs into numb and senseless clubs beating at the surface. There's something ahead, like some gigantic washing machine about to swallow me whole. This is it. Dig it in, *everything you got.*

I'm neither gaining nor losing ground, locked in an aquatic wrestle. My arms weaken, my breath is ragged. I'm losing the fight, resorting to a pathetic doggy paddle, barely keeping my head above water. I'm about to sink into the gloomy pit of despair, taking in a mouthful of froth, when my feet find purchase. I just manage to stand on the bottom and wade to the bank.

Exhausted, I lie face down, incapable of moving. I allow myself to just be still – the cold stones on the side of my face, life slowly returning to my limbs. I think of Lincoln. Amongst the explosion of airbags and turbulence, there was no way of rescuing him. I was barely lucky to escape the tomb of the sinking camper.

I roll onto my back and squint up at the clouds. They clear away like spectators leaving the stadium. I smile insanely, overwhelmed and exhilarated by this one primal thought, hidden under layers of distraction, societal pressure, relationships, an eternity of choices good and bad, this one precious sense I had forgotten until it was almost gone. *I'm alive.* I want to bottle this thought and have it fed into me on a slow drip.

Someone's yelling.

It's hard to detect, but it's coming from upstream – an SOS. I get to my feet, stagger over boulders, warming my body into a steady rhythm of hopping from rock to rock. Further up I make out a lone figure stranded in the centre of the river, rapids surging on either side, and an enormous undercut of rock waiting where the river bends. As I get closer, I can see he's clinging to the corner of the camper jutting out of the water. Suddenly I'm not sure if I want to be seen but it's too late. He's spotted me already – his face drenched in fear. He's yelling something. Something about a rope inside his car.

I'm already moving, scrambling up the steep incline of boulders to where his Falcon's parked. I can't watch a man drown, can't bear to see another face starved of oxygen. I don't stop to think what this might mean. This is just about a person drowning and another trying to prevent it from happening.

I pick up a rock and smash the side window of the Falcon, open the front door, click the boot. I recoil at what I find inside. I pick out the rope, sling it over my shoulder, try to ignore the spade, the hacksaw and hammer, the bag of lime. Those items don't exist. Because if they did exist then I'm a complete fool to do what I'm doing.

I coil one end of the rope into a small, easy to throw bundle. I swing my arm and cast the rope out. Hohepa's look of hope evaporates as it falls short. I draw it back, re-coil the end. It's heavier now, waterlogged, perhaps easier to throw. I take a run up and give it my all. The rope sails well past him and he lunges at it, getting a grip with both hands. We're connected, the rope goes taut, but I'm off balance. The line slips through my hands and he's adrift from the wreckage, desperately trying to keep his head above water. I dig in my heels, wrap the line around my forearm. He goes under, hooked on like some big game fish, and pops up further downstream, gasping. He's closing in on the bank. Soon he'll find his feet and be standing in front of me. I hesitate. Last chance to let go. But then it would be murder, wouldn't it? The line goes slack. He's standing. Not sure whether to run or help. He could make it from there. He looks exhausted, grabbing hold of the rock. But then I'm exhausted too, and if I ran, how far would I really get? Nope, I've already made this choice, may as well follow it through.

Where he's positioned, he has a little way to climb before he's completely out of danger. He's desperately trying to get his fat arse up the rock, but each time he steps up he slides back, cursing. I bundle the rope and find a tree at the top of the incline. I hastily knot the rope at incremental spaces for easy grips, and tie it off at the base of the trunk. I throw the end down to Hohepa. He grabs it greedily. It's aiding his climb pretty well. He heaves and splutters, gaining height. As he gets closer, I notice a nasty bruised swelling to one side of his face, where he must have got slammed on impact. "You can do it!" I say. Then I check myself – what the fuck are you saying? You're giving words of encouragement to a guy who has brought tools in the boot of his car to chop you into pieces and bury you. Are you sure you want this? I try to shake the grim thought. This is a rescue, I tell myself. A straight-up rescue. Then I feel a hard lump wedged in my pocket and it gives me an idea. Call it an insurance policy.

He's about two thirds up, within earshot, when I pull out the pocketknife. "Hey!" I call out.

He stops, looks up. His breath catches when he sees the knife blade resting against the rope.

"Now that I've got your attention, you might want to hear what I've got to say."

"You haven't got the balls," he says, spitting, and continues climbing.

"Oh yeah!" I slice at the rope, but only deep enough so the sheath pulls apart and splays out in threads. The inside core is still intact, but he doesn't know that. He stops, looks up at me properly this time.

"One more cut and you'll fall back on those rocks. I promise you. You want that?"

He hesitates, like it's the hardest thing he's ever had to do. "Spit it out."

"Good. Because how I see it, I've rescued your sorry arse. So, you could say we're even. More than even. I walk away from this not owing you anything. You get my drift?"

He nods. "Sure thing." He reaches for the next knot.

"Wait! How do I know you mean it?"

He looks away momentarily, smiles. "I wasn't even going to hurt you anyway, Kurt, just scare you a bit. It was Lincoln I wanted. You're just small fry."

"Yeah, well, what I want to know is, what's going to happen when you're up here next to me? I want to know we've got a solid deal here. I will promise you I won't breathe a word to anyone after all this is over, not a soul. I swear on my mother's grave." I pause. "Now I want you to do the same."

"All right, whatever. I swear on *my* mother's grave."

I lower the knife, so it's almost touching the core. "That doesn't sound convincing. How do I know you even have a mother?"

"What do ya mean?"

"Well, you could have been, I don't know, brought up by some foster mum, which technically wouldn't count."

"I have a mother, motherfucker!"

"What's her name?"

"Gloria."

"Oh yeah? She sounds too nice. How did you turn out so bad?"

"I've changed my mind."

"About what?"

"I think I *will* kill you when I get up there." He reaches again to start his climb, knuckles whitening on the rope. I motion the knife again, threatening to cut him loose. He stops. "All right, I'm fucking kidding. I won't lay a finger. We've got a deal. I swear on it. I even swear on my patch, okay?"

I stare into his eyes and for the first time it feels like we're on an equal footing.

"What about that tattoo on your forehead? That must be pretty important to you. Swear on that and we've got a deal."

He laughs. "What, you think I got this done on purpose? I was comatose at my stag party. It was a prank."

"You're married?"

"Yeah, I'm fucking married, with kids."

"Okay, climb away." I step back and watch him belly flop on the ledge like a beached whale. He lies in front of me, limbs splayed out. My thoughts return to Lincoln.

The camper is still protruding from the water. Displacement theory tells me there's likely air trapped under that corner, and Lincoln could be right behind it sucking in his last breaths, that's if he managed to rip himself free from the steering wheel. There's a chance; it may be small, but I have to try. I untie the rope, bunch it in my arms and head upstream of the camper. I need to anchor the rope somehow. There's no tree in sight close enough to make this work. Hohepa is up on his feet now, limping over the rocks. "What the fuck are you doing?" he yells.

"I need you to hold the rope. I'm going in." I tie a bowline around my waist. "You're nuts," he says. "You want to drown?"

I look at him. "Lincoln might be in there, alive. I need to check it out." I'm about to wade in when I feel a tug on the line, stopping me from going further. "You're not going in, Kurt. If he is alive, he won't be much longer. And I want to keep it that way."

I swing around, "You arsehole!"

He rushes me, grabs hold of the scruff of my shirt, brings his face right up to mine so that I can feel his words spit. "Our deal is good. Don't make me break it!"

"But... we gotta try!"

He squeezes me tighter. "Listen. I want him dead. Dead as a dodo. You get?"

I don't nod. Just stand there. He lets go.

"Now, tell me. Did you see him trying to get out, free himself from the wheel or something?"

"Are you kidding? He had his hand clamped on. You made sure of that, remember?" I look out at the river, searchingly.

He nods. "Yeah, good job too." He pats me on the shoulder, by way of consolation. "You've got to understand he had it coming. It's just the way it is in our business." He turns in the direction of the car. "You coming, maggot? I'll give you a lift back."

I sigh, take one last look at the camper. It's moving, but what hope I have in that second is extinguished as it keels over submerging completely. I close my eyes and turn uphill towards the car.

I don't know what makes me turn and glance over my shoulder one last time, but I do and it makes all the difference, putting to rest a future of eternal worry and self-doubt – did I do everything I could? Everything is bound together in a perfect whole that I can finally swallow. Lincoln's face, just a split second, peers over a large boulder on the other side of the river. Our eyes meet. I don't react, just flick out my thumb casually. Thumbs up. I see him grin and I turn away. Hohepa hasn't noticed a thing.

62

This is good. This is very good and yet I'm completely lost.

Geographically I'm in Wanaka, sitting at the lakeside edge with silhouetted mountains waiting to be printed onto a picture postcard. I should be grateful. Hohepa agreed to drop by the Nissan so I could retrieve my pack. I had to tell him I didn't know how to drive since he got suspicious why I wouldn't take the car for myself. He shook his head in disbelief and dropped me off here instead. I haven't moved, except to purchase a dozen beers that I've been drinking steadily since I arrived here.

It's weird. Before I had some direction, even if it was only for survival. Suddenly the pressure is off and reality is back – depleted funds, no job, no career prospects. The only beacon of light is Jasmine. It was such a magic night but now I'm starting to doubt whether she felt the same or if I just imagined it. What if I show up and she just stares at me, not believing that I would actually stalk her all the way to Dunedin. I should probably phone her first, test the waters. Remembering my copy of *Slaughterhouse-Five* and her number scrawled inside, I dig into my pack, upend the whole thing and rifle through the contents of scrunched up clothes and bits of climbing gear. Could this be the sum of my life? It wouldn't be so bad if I still had the book. But with that gone I see very little value. Shit, it must have slipped out. There goes Jas.

I'm left with four cans of beer which I drain in the time the sun lowers in the sky, blinding me. I close my eyes, study the back of my eyelids – blood orange – and sense the weight of choices unravelling into the future, and if only I could see past the blinding light, I'd know which way to turn, but it's hot and unrelenting. I open my eyes and surrender, drunk before the sun.

63

Receipts for memories. That's all I have when I wake the next day in a backpacker and concede that my brain has been taken for a joy ride – stripped, completely gutted, then put back into my skull. Christ, I can feel it rattling around in there like a dried-up walnut.

Eftpos receipts are the only evidence I have of last night. Wherever this Apartment One bar was, I might never know. But there's proof I was there between one and four in the morning, clocking up rounds of drinks at forty to fifty dollars a pop. The total of last night is around four hundred dollars. A frightening, depressing thought.

On the back of the receipts, I find scribbling – *my* handwriting. I can only guess these words were meant to be profound and mystic. I'm scratching my head as to what they could possibly mean. *Words connected to make a sentence; I lost my mind in Takaka, I'm still looking for it in Wanaka.*

I really need to get my shit together. Beginning with hydration, eating something, general self-care, then I can function, come up with some kind of direction. I stand up out of bed, lightheaded, giddy, steady myself against the wall.

That afternoon I'm sitting at a table entangled with puzzles – puzzles with strings, puzzles with loops and wires and interconnecting blocks. I've become fixated by this cube puzzle. Six pieces of various wooden shapes somehow connect to form a solid cube. It has taken on a whole new meaning for me to solve this damn puzzle since I've already spent close to an hour on it. Normally I would've given up if it wasn't for the therapeutic distraction from the bigger overarching puzzle – my life. Turns out Puzzling World is ideal for hangovers, a place to balance the electrolytes, hydrate the walnut.

The final piece slots into place and I spin the cube around to admire all the sides before putting it down.

I'm still lost.

I complete the outdoor maze and stop to stare at the gallery of Escher prints – I can almost empathise with the small stubby men trapped in an absurd Escher world. Everything makes sense from one perspective then morphs into paradox.

I'm still lost.

There are the inversed faces of Albert Einstein that, with a gestalt switch in your brain, begin to protrude out in three dimensions. But my favourite, for whatever reason, is the staircase seat that when you sit down, you're moving up the stairs defying gravity. I repeat it a dozen times, hogging it from kids waiting in queue. It's addictive. I want to be on this all day, keeping me in temporary limbo so that I don't have to deal with the real effect of gravity that at some point will send me crashing. But that's the point, isn't it? To return to Earth after being in space so long you've forgotten what it's like to breathe normal air. I just need to decide on something and stick with it. I think Jas said that? Dunedin is the closest city and my best bet to make my remaining funds last. If I stay here, I'd barely last a week. In Dunnes I could stretch it out for a month on a tight budget.

That's it then. I hop off the antigravity seat and land firmly on the ground.

64

After a four-hour bus ride the next day, I'm descending into Dunedin city. I was expecting grey depressing weather. But when I step off the bus and retrieve my pack, I'm faced with a crisp blue afternoon, no wind and a gothic city of Victorian architecture. It's unusually quiet here for the centre of town. People move around like they're on holiday.

I checked into a backpacker half way along Princes Street – a converted rundown mansion – a relic of the gold rush. The guy running it made me pay upfront because I was Kiwi. "Foreigners," he said. "They always pay. Don't take offence. But it's always the locals that are unreliable."

I didn't sweat it. I'm just glad to be in Dunnes, in this bar which the backpacker guy recommended. Tuesday is two-dollar pint night at Arc Café. Macs beer on tap, brimming with goodness and only two smackaroonies the whole evening.

There's a guy sitting across from me in the booth – long greasy hair, glasses, eighties leather jacket. I decide he must fit the local profile. "You from Dunedin?" I ask.

He looks up from his beer, nods. "Yeah, been living here for a few years. Where're you from?"

Already this conversation seems different from being in Auckland. In the big smoke, you'd only get a weird look from striking up a conversation with a stranger. This guy actually seems genuinely interested in talking. "I'm from nowhere," I say. "But I'm thinking about being from Dunedin. I take it you rate this place?"

"Since I was a first year."

"And how long ago was that, I hope you don't mind me asking?"

He looks down into his beer. "Nineteen-eighty-nine. And I'm still studying."

I lean forward. "What? How's that possible?"

He takes a sip of his beer, delicately places the glass on the table. "Started with a BA in English lit, ended up doing a double degree, one in honours, then master's. Took a year off and tried to start up a band – The Dead Lentils – back when people were still talking about 'the Dunedin sound'. We couldn't produce anything decent, so I went back and started on my PhD." He takes a heavy swig of his beer, spills a little, wipes his mouth with his sleeve. "I have found that critiquing Emmanuel Kant's critique of pure reason is a real exercise in stamina."

"No shit," I say, nodding. "It makes my grad degree seem like a day pass compared to your effort." I pause, take a sip of beer. "How do you stay motivated?"

He laughs. "I don't. I procrastinate."

This guy seems all right so I shout him a beer and we get talking about the Dunedin sound that was once an empire of bands – The Chills, The Clean, The Verlaines –

all shaping NZ music in the eighties. He tells me the sound doesn't exist anymore but the remnants are still burned into the city.

One piece of advice he gives me before the evening ends is not to get a flat near the campus. Mattress fires, juvenile chaos and overpriced, dank hovels that aren't even worth looking at. "Head just out of town," he suggests. "Try Ravensbourne. A bit shady, but quiet and cheap."

I hold onto that advice the next day and survey the newspaper for flatmates wanted. There are a couple of ads for Ravensbourne. I phone one of them. A professional sounding lady answers, presumably the agent. She says the room has French doors, plenty of sun. I can view it this afternoon.

65

The place is relatively easy to find. Slightly elevated, on the corner of two crossroads and shielded by a tall conifer hedge. I walk down the gravel drive that opens out to a large villa. In the carport is a blue Mazda convertible, presumably the agent's. I knock on the door, try to tidy myself up, patting down my hair, tucking my shirt in. The door opens. She is perhaps in her late twenties, quite young for an agent and dressed in a snug two-piece business suit. She looks professional. When she smiles I notice freshly applied lipstick. "Hi, you must be Kurt. Please, come in." Slightly intimidated, I dump my pack on the porch and follow her as she takes me on a tour through the house. A voice in my head is telling me there's no way I'm going to get this place – it's too nice. Elegant wood trimmings, polished floors, rooms all furnished, real paintings on the walls – it's as if I'm invading someone's private home. I'm trying to prepare in my head what I'm going to say when she asks what I do for a living. My unkempt appearance doesn't really instil much credibility.

"As you can see," she says, bending to lift the sash window, "there's a pleasant view of the harbour from the kitchen." I nod as she glances back at me. "And what do you do, Kurt, may I ask?"

"Huh?"

She straightens, adjusts her suit jacket. "You know, what are you interested in, what makes you tick?" She walks over to the stove and surprises me by igniting the gas hob.

"Um… I'm, well… looking for a job at the moment." *Am I? Is that why I'm here?*

She pulls open a draw, takes out two butter knives, blackened at the ends. "You smoke weed?"

Maybe I'm hearing voices. Did she actually say that? "Um, pardon?"

She looks straight at me, her eyes heavy with confidence. "I should let you know, I smoke weed, regularly. If you're going to live with me, I think you ought to know that."

Thoughts are ticking over; I nod quickly. "Sure, I'm partial to a bit of weed." I pause. "So, is this, like, your own place or something?"

She shakes her head as she removes a bud from a tiny wooden box. "This is a house-sitting arrangement. A professor at the university offered it to me while he's away on sabbatical."

I nod, looking around. "Oh, I see… nice place."

She rolls four tiny balls of head and lines them up on a chopping board. "He doesn't know I'm getting in flatmates. That's why the rent is so cheap." The knives on the stove start to glow red hot. "So, Kurt, do you know how to drive?"

"Um, to be honest I don't have a driver's license."

She laughs. "No, I mean, do you know how to drive a spot?"

"Oh, that. Yeah, I'm an expert in spotting."

She smiles, picks up the funnel. "Tell you what. If you do this right, I'll give you the room. Agreed?"

"Sure," I say, not sure whether she's joking.

I revise the technique in my head. The knives must be red hot. Check. With the right knife, ever so carefully, I press it onto the ball of weed – this sticks to the knife blade without burning it which wastes the smoke. Then expediently, but without panic, I press the ball between the hottest points of the knives directly under the funnel, grinding them together to extract the residue, making sure at the same time not to nick the funnel with the knives, which can give off a very unpleasant after taste.

The spot combusts perfectly, filling the funnel with thick white smoke. She inhales in one hit, holds it in deep and releases a hazy cloud.

"Well, did I get the room?"

She smiles, eyes blazing. "With honours."

66

Things are looking up. I'm not dead. I'm not being hunted down. These last few days I am almost leading a normal life. A life with regular choices – what to eat, when to go to sleep, what will I do for money? Shall I go on the dole or get some kind of regular job? Perhaps I could return to study, do my master's? These are all choices I seem to appreciate now, whereas before I would've felt they were excruciatingly mundane. Just pick something and stick with it. I won't die, nothing really bad will happen. At worst I might fail, and that I can live with.

I'm sitting in Governors Café, by the window, looking out at George Street and the gothic spire of Knox Church spiking the still grey sky. I think of Lincoln as I lift a mug of black filter coffee to my lips – cheap, bitter, priced right for my budget. He's out there somewhere, riding his choice to its full conclusion.

Good luck and farewell.

I think of those poor bastards who decided to get into a wheelie bin last night and rode it down Baldwin Street – unofficially the steepest street in the world. According to the newspaper, these two first-year students died on impact when they hit a trailer laden with concrete. The weird thing is I could imagine myself thinking it would be a good idea too, a couple of months ago. This is the lethal rush of danger I really don't need anymore.

Good luck and farewell.

I'm at the dregs of my coffee, contemplating my next move, when a girl I recognise walks by the window. She's listening to her Discman and doesn't hear me banging on the glass. I exit Governors in a flash. I'm running. My God, am I in some cliché movie ending? Slow down, don't embarrass yourself, just a good solid walk will do. "Jasmine!" But still, she doesn't hear me. I catch up to her, tap her on the shoulder.

She spins around, startled. She's not smiling yet, even though I am. She removes one of her earbuds. "Kurt, my God!" She beams. I'm not sure whether to hug her. I want to, but restrain myself. Maybe she's changed her mind. Maybe she's about to tell me she's met someone else.

"I'm here," I say, out of breath. "In Dunedin."

She smiles. "So you are."

I move in for the hug. It's awkward, hesitant, standing there in the middle of the footpath with people walking by, but we connect and she squeezes me tight, just enough for me to know we're still good.

"Great that you're here," she says.

I'm looking over her shoulder. I want to tell her I've missed her, but what I'm seeing up ahead has paralysed the speech centre of my brain. There's a red Skoda with its blinker on, indicating to pull out. On the rear window is a

'For Sale' sign. The number plate matches. I manage to form words robotically. "I… I'm, glad to see you too."

She releases her arms. "Hey, listen to this." She plugs the other earbud into my ear, so now we're both listening. The blinker is still indicating right, waiting for a gap in the traffic. "Can you guess what song this is?"

I want to say Mazzy Star. I want to tell her, *Fade into You.*